Wash your needless soda down as Anton

for Kip

Wash your needless soda down as Anton

ISBN: 978-1-943661-08-4

Wash your needless soda down as Anton is Issue Three of *4ink7,* a literary journal that is a book. Individually, all rights revert to the authors upon publication. The title is taken from Sally Roundhouse's "Incantation for the Drought."

Printed in the USA

4ink7
PO BOX 4945
Chattanooga, TN 37405

Editor: Russell Helms
Associate Editor: Hannah Sandoval

Cover and text design: 47 Journals

Contents

Sybil Baker

Schemers

One day, during the seventies when I was around ten, my brothers and I discovered a large house in the middle of a field not far from where we lived. Our family had moved from our little starter home in Florissant, Missouri, to a more spacious two-story colonial on the edge of the suburbs of Fairfax, Virginia. Behind our house was a small forest and beyond that a field where we discovered the abandoned house, sprawling and surrounded by dead overgrown grass.

We pushed the door open and walked in. Right away we could see that a family had lived there and had left the house in a hurry. The couches and chairs were still arranged in the living room as if the family were about to watch TV or entertain guests. Upstairs, the bedrooms still had dressers and bedspreads. The windows were framed by gauzy curtains. Clothes were still hanging and folded in closets and dressers containing bellbottoms and bright scarves and beaded tops with sleeves that flared out. Back downstairs in the family room, we found schoolbooks with homework. But what remains imprinted in my mind were the *Ebony* magazines stacked on the coffee table, waiting to be read.

I still wonder what it was that made them go.

We were schemers, my husband Rowan and I. I suspect it came from our expatriate lifestyle in Seoul, where we met, and our desire to see a world beyond the one we knew. The more you see of the world the more you know how precarious it all is, governments, economies, systems. Rowan—whose family had emigrated from South Africa to Canada, and subsequently, through bad luck and bad decisions, had lost all of their money—felt the precariousness of the world even more deeply than I did. Until I'd moved to South Korea in 1995, my life had been solidly and predictably American middle class. But, my parents had grown up under the cloud of the Depression, and our family did not waste. My mother reused the brown paper bags my dad carried his lunch in to work. My dad carpeted our house, installed cabinets and worked on our ever-aging cars. We had a garden and canned the tomatoes and beans we didn't eat. Even when he no longer needed to, my dad would make a meal of the samples offered at the grocery store. He went to retirement investment seminars simply for the free steak dinners.

My dad was raised in subsistence-level poverty working on the family's small cotton farm in Possum Valley, Arkansas. While in the Navy in the early 1950s, he'd seen dead bodies in the gutters of pre-Maoist China and children begging along the streets of Manila. Traveling through Mongolia, Cambodia, and Indonesia, I'd witnessed countries in extreme poverty and upheaval, countries that had once been empires. One day, perhaps in our lifetime, our civilization, too, would fall. Rowan and I thought, if we planned properly, we might be able to survive it.

Often at night in our tiny apartment in Seoul, after a drink or two, we'd come up with some cramped, crazy version of the American Dream: we would make money flipping houses, even though we didn't possess basic handyman skills; we'd quit our jobs and move to Dubai where we'd rake in so much dough we could retire early on an unnamed island; or we'd save just enough money to survive in a hut in some very cheap country until the apocalypse caught up with us. We were working toward an image more than an idea: Rowan and me, framed by two battered suitcases, waving from a car or a boat or a plane whisking us away from the madness of the world. I'd never moved beyond that image, failing to imagine what I'd do once we'd settled into a bamboo hut and battled mosquitoes and strange customs, with no bookstore on the island and no WiFi to download all those books I was finally going to read. Imagining our life beyond the moment we waved goodbye was for later. The important thing was to quit the crazy modern world and its superficial distractions on our own terms.

Some of our schemes had actually worked. In 2007, we bought a house right off the internet. At that time we'd been plotting to work ten more years in Korea and then retire on the nameless island. Then my father, who lived in North Carolina, was diagnosed with terminal cancer. I spent the first months of 2007, my semeste break, helping my mom take care of him, driving him to his doctor and chemo appointments. When I saw through my graduate alumni network an advertisement for the last tenure-track-creative-writing-job-in-America-for-someone-who-hadn't-published-a-book at a university six hours from where my parents lived, I applied. I didn't believe in fate, but this job felt like it was meant for me to be closer to my mother after my father's imminent death.

As soon as I was offered the position, I learned the university had exactly one remaining forgivable home loan for employees who bought a house in the rapidly gentrifying Martin Luther King neighborhood near campus. Rowan and I were determined to get that loan, so we bought a newish house that looked appealing in the photos we viewed online in Seoul.

In July 2007, we left my dying father in North Carolina and drove my aunt's trailer packed with family furniture no one else wanted to our new house, opened the door and walked in for the first time. The house had large windows, wood floors, and a front porch with a view of the mountains. We loved it even more in real life. The owner, a young white guy, had taken a job in North Carolina and was ready to sell.

For the next seven years we would sit on our porch at night with our neighbors George and Anita and watch people bike past to the convenience store a few blocks from us, then return with a bag of something (beer? milk? potato chips?) propped between the handlebars. Behind the bicyclists was a freight train station, and beyond that was the Chattanooga National Cemetery, where veterans of our many wars were buried. Beyond that was the horizon of Lookout Mountain, where much bigger, older, and more expensive houses offered views of the river and city below. I wondered what they thought, if anything, when they looked at us, that if all we were to them were smudges of dark and light.

Across from our house were the Chattanooga Transportation Authority and a two-story brick building, behind them were the train tracks. On the second floor of the building were a few apartments. On the first floor of the building, a bar opened on weekends. Fridays and Saturdays the empty parking lot of the Transportation Authority filled. From the cars emerged the bar's clientele: older blacks wearing brimmed hats and dinner jackets and brightly colored dresses and high heels. The bar must have been soundproofed because from our bedroom balcony we only heard a slip of music, mostly soul and R&B, when someone was entering or exiting.

Occasionally at closing time a bit of street drama might

erupt—fighting couples, loud drunken conversations, minor dis-
agreements—and Rowan and I would watch from our balcony with
bemused interest until the customers disappeared back to their
own neighborhoods. In our own way we were just like the people
on Lookout Mountain, watching from our lighted perch, safe and
removed from the action below.

One late Friday afternoon, after living in our house for about six
months, Rowan and I walked over to the bar to introduce ourselves.
On the door to the bar was a sign saying people under the age of
thirty were not allowed in. Being over thirty, we opened the door.

A barrel chested man and a woman in tight leather pants, large
hoop earrings, and close-cropped white hair were stocking the
fridge with 40s behind the bar. The man, named Mike, was owner
of the bar, which, for reasons still not clear to me, was called Mike's
Place. When we told him we lived across the street, he invited us
to come back that evening or any other time. He told us he wanted
his bar to be "international." In our neighborhood, international,
I realized, meant Mike was okay with allowing white folks into his
black bar.

When we returned that evening, Mike ran over from around the
bar and embraced us, leading us to one of the card tables near the
dance floor. Men wore fedoras and porkpie hats and suits accent-
ed with brightly colored shirts. The women had done-up hair and
sparkly dresses and long fake fingernails that clutched proper pock-
etbooks. Guys felt sorry for me and asked me to dance. They tried
to help me. *Girl, you got to loosen up.* But even though we returned
many times, I never could, not the way they wanted me to. I felt too
old, too uptight, too self-conscious. Too white.

We had such a good time that night dancing and drinking and
talking, that we continued to return about once a month. Despite
some troubles (parking issues, employees stealing inventory, a
shooting by a customer right after closing), the bar remained open
and popular until the fall of 2010, when, without fanfare, it did not
open one night. For months afterward, cars would slow down by the
shutdown bar, not having got the word that it had closed. A year
later I ran into Mike at the Bessie Smith Strut, and he told me he'd
shut the place down because he was afraid of having a heart attack.
Keeping the bar open was taking a toll on his health.

I wondered what might have happened if Mike had been able to expand and develop the club the way he'd wanted, to make it "international." I wonder what might have happened if he'd been white, or been given some kind of support to turn his club into something that thrived. But that was not to be. His dream, in the end, cost too much, emotionally and financially.

After My Uncle's Place closed, Rowan and I started a garden with George and Anita, harvesting tomatoes, cucumbers, hot peppers, and lettuce. We bought silver coins in case the apocalypse happened sooner than we'd planned, which we hid in a shoebox in our attic. Finally, with the forgivable loan forgiven and a substantial down payment from the money we'd saved in Korea, we'd managed to aggressively pay down our mortgage. Six years after we'd bought it, we owned our house free and clear. Freed up with cash, we started scheming again.

We decided to rent out the MLK house and bought a historic fixer-upper on the other side of campus by the Tennessee River and running trail. For the first six months we lived with construction workers and asbestos and lead paint abatement and ceilings that had fallen in from clogged plumbing. We brushed our teeth in the kitchen sink and showered at the gym. We spent our free time peeling off yellowed daisy dotted wallpaper I detested and then painting the walls a noncontroversial off-white. A year later, our "new" old house was problematic but livable, and our house in MLK was still being successfully rented out to university students.

But schemers are never satisfied with what they have, and one afternoon, I started surfing Zillow again, and that was when I spotted a boarded up cottage on MLK a few blocks from a convenience store, within walking distance to campus, going for 20k. From the photos of the house's exterior, it didn't look irredeemable. In our experience, paint jobs and regular lawn maintenance worked wonders. We'd done both with the MLK rental property and our current house, which was now increasing in value. If we bought another property and fixed it up, we could be like those aspirational real estate types on reality TV.

There'd be some sacrifice. We'd have to sell our silver coins as well as our only car, but we'd get around on foot, take the bus, ride bikes, just like poor people and hipsters. I showed the listing to

Rowan, and we decided to check the house out on our own before calling our realtor.

That afternoon we walked over to our old neighborhood and found the house on a little-used side street. We stood in the middle of the crumbling road, trying to assess not only the house's damage but its possibility for redemption. Empty beer cans and plastic drink bottles pockmarked the yard's waist-high weeds. On the front porch lay an inch-thick sponge mattress covered with a rumpled blanket and tree fallings. That porch, despite its rotting wood and spreading cobwebs, was still someone's sometime shelter. In the back, the house was propped up with stacks of bricks where the foundation had sagged. The roof was missing tiles and sloped awkwardly. The chipped and fading exterior needed several fresh coats of paint. The doors and windows were hidden with splintery cracked boards. But until we could go inside, we wouldn't know whether we could save the house or not.

We walked back to the road and surveyed the house again. We didn't have to rent it out to students. We could turn it into a private club in the spirit of My Uncle's Place, where we'd meet up with our friends and smoke and drink and play whatever music we wanted, without having to deal with the increasing soullessness of the local bar scene. Cell phones and people bothered by secondhand smoke would be banned. We'd have a red neon sign on the door with its name blazing away: RJ's Rock'n'Roll Bar.

We were discussing if our bar would be a members-only venue, when we heard our names being called from the top of the street. Like an apparition, our friend and former neighbor, George, who had been on his way to the convenience store to buy cigarettes, loped toward us. After we hugged, we told him of our scheme to buy the house in cash and then rent it to students or turn it into a bar for our friends.

George said he was cool with our plans, and that he'd like to do something like that himself, before the "whites bought everything up." Even though Rowan and I were white and had bought a house in his neighborhood, he felt we were on his side. Just like Mike's "international" was code for "white people," "whites" was code for "gentrifiers." George was a fellow schemer, and we'd spent many nights discussing the buildings we'd buy, the businesses we'd open, the rooms we would fix up. George often talked of the bar he'd run for several years on MLK, The Chameleon, until right before the millennium, he drove away one night to LA, not returning until years later. I imagined that The Chameleon, integrated, with its poetry nights and live jazz, was what Mike had wanted his bar to be, and what RJ's Rock'n'Roll bar could become.

George wished us luck and we promised to get together soon. Before he made it to the top of the hill, I'd already turned toward the run-down house, wondering if we could make this work.

A few days later, we met our realtor in front of the house. Her seven-month-old son, still sleepy-eyed, was comfortably swaddled at her chest. There was no lockbox, so our realtor called someone to remove the boards that blocked the door. We waited for about ten minutes, but when nobody arrived, we pried the boards back ourselves. We pushed the door open and walked in.

I wondered if this time my scheming had gone too far. Boards blocked the windows, making it hard to see what was in front of me. Someone turned on their cell phone flashlight to illuminated the rotted boards, broken bits of furniture, electric wires snaking medusa-like from holes in the walls. Whatever had been worth something—appliances, copper wire, fixtures—had long been hauled away.

Just outside on the buckling front porch, the spongy mattress soaked up the late summer sun. I turned back to the blocked front door, ready to walk away, to abandon my ambition to fix this unfixable house.

But Rowan and our realtor and her baby swaddled to her chest were already moving toward the kitchen. Maybe the rest of the house wasn't that bad. Maybe we could still turn things around. I took another step forward and waited for my eyes to adjust to a world without light.

Our realtor's son was quiet. Cuddled against his mother, he probably discerned a few intriguing shapes enveloped in a cooling darkness. I felt terrible that her baby was here, afraid that this scene of destruction and desolation would imprint on him in some dark, inexorable way.

We carefully treaded from the living room to the kitchen. Stripped of counters and appliances, it was just a space with falling boards and ripped walls. Perversely, stacked on the floor were piles of sheetrock, harkening to a more optimistic time when someone had started framing the area, perhaps looking to rebuild the house. In that same area someone had started work on a dropped ceiling, a project that seemed to be borderline delusional given the bigger issues of the house.

Past the kitchen was a small bedroom, in which someone (the same person sleeping outside?) had recently been living. The mattress, covered in a few tangled, stained sheets was surrounded by empty 40s, fast food wrappers, crumpled paper, waxy soft drink cups.

The bathroom floor was unstable, sinking from the falling foundation. A stiff towel was stuffed in the hole where a toilet had been to keep the sewage smells from rising. I circumvented the bathroom and walked into the last room.

The long abandoned home of my father's family in Possum Valley, Arkansas, with its depression-era structure was not any larger than the house I was in at the moment. My father's house was on a cotton farm and had no electricity or plumbing. When I was twelve we returned to the old family home. I remember walking through the spent cotton fields, where my father used to watch the sky for planes, pretending he was flying to some unknown state or country. Inside his old house, almost collapsed, the walls were lined with tea-colored flowered wallpaper. The peeled strips looked like baby's curls. I knew the wallpaper's main purpose was to keep the wind out, but even so, I admired the aspirational sophistication of the delicate rose pattern.

There was no aspirational wallpaper in this last room of the this empty house, only notes of hopelessness magic-markered on spotted walls in a room littered with broken pieces of things that could never be put back together. I read the messages quickly, and I do not remember the words. I only remember the content: that life had not turned out as planned, and in fact life had taken people to a dark empty room from which they'd never escape. They could have been notes of suicide. They could have been ramblings of a junkie. The f-word was used like a comma. They were the cries of people who'd reached the end of the line.

It was time for me to go.

As I approached the door to leave the dilapidated house, I heard someone calling to us, as if in some alternate world, this was our house, and someone had come "visiting." They were father and son, the ones who were supposed to have let us in thirty minutes before. They apologized for being late. The father, in his sixties or seventies, wore a red "I love Jesus" baseball hat, and was earnestly smoking a cigarette, almost purposely blowing clouds toward the baby's placid face. After a while, we figured out he was—or had been—the home-owner.

They were congenial enough, happy to strike up a conversation with strangers, the way Tennesseans are inclined to do. The old man solved one mystery after another about the house. A few years ago he had started fixing it up, but there was only so much an old man could do, he said. The leftover drywall and ceiling was his. He seemed proud of the house, said that a lot could be done with it. He said, compared to others he'd seen, this one was not bad. His son said that this house, along with some other properties (including the one next door, still inhabited, with two churning AC window units on each side, like dark, fixed eyes), had been bought up by a woman in Texas who wanted to sell them to the highest bidder. When they sold, whoever was living in them would be kicked out.

We finished our conversation, and like good Southern hosts, we waved goodbye from the sunken porch, sending father and son on their way.

In the mornings, when my brothers and I were young in our new suburban neighborhood, we'd wait for my father, in suit and tie, to finish his breakfast so that we could run to the bay window in the living room and wave goodbye to him as he backed out of our drive-way, heading to his white-collar job working for a defense contrac-tor. I can see us, three tow-headed kids, hands pressed against the window, sending him off not with fear but with fanfare because we knew that every evening he would return.

One day someone, probably a white person, would buy that house and erase those messages off those walls. That white person was not going to be me.

That fall of 2014, after we gave up our scheme to sell our car to buy that house of despair, I looked up my old childhood house in Florissant, Missouri, a few miles from Ferguson, on Zillow. Built in

1956, the house was just over a decade old when my parents sold it in 1968. Now, in 2014, the listing says, "With a little TLC, this would make a great family home." The house, a 1,200 square foot ranch home, last sold on December 31, 2012, for $36,098, not much more than that house of despair I'd momentarily dreamed of buying.

I wondered if the inside of my childhood home would look the way I remembered it. The narrow hall that led to my bedroom where an evil red clown on the wall threatened me at night. The table where my baby brother peed on me while I watched my father change his diaper. The chair in the kitchen I'd sit in to watch the *Three Stooges* on our tiny black and white TV and eat M&Ms from a cup. Until I got my tonsils out when I was four, I was often sick in that house, not allowed to go to church or the grocery store, so my life didn't extend beyond our tiny cul-de-sac of a street. But it was enough. When I was well, the house opened onto a street where everything was possible. I would meet my neighbor friends and we would ride our tricycles and wear plastic jewelry that sparkled and gossip about whatever three-year-olds gossiped about. On the best days my mom would fix me my favorite sandwich, butter and ketch-up on white bread, and I'd watch in awe as my five-year-old neighbor rode his banana-seat bike without training wheels down our street.

But the best memory of that time was when in the summer evenings a city truck would spew DDT to kill the mosquitoes, fat and fertile, the white clouds thick in the humid air. As our parents watched from their lawns, my neighbor friends and I, all under five years old, chased each other in those silvery puffs, pretending to be lost in the fog or angels floating in heaven.

When I was four, after my tonsils were cut out and I no longer was sick, my dad, an engineer, got a better job with a better home in a better place in Virginia. Our Florissant starter home was temporary, just a step on the ladder to white-collar success. I remember sitting in the station wagon, waving goodbye to that first house. But I wasn't sad, I didn't cry. After all, our new house and yard would be bigger and better. Unlike Rowan, unlike Mike, unlike George, unlike the man with the Jesus hat, unlike the person who had written words of despair on those crumbling bedroom walls, unlike the family who had optimistically stacked their *Ebony* magazines as if they had all the time in the world, unlike Michael Brown, shot a few miles

from where I was born, unlike them, this was the America I knew.
Like my dad, so far from Possum Valley, I was going somewhere.
   I couldn't imagine anyone or anything trying to stop me.
   I couldn't imagine not wanting to wave goodbye.

Terry Barr

Scissors, Paper, Brick

Somewhere in the middle of last week, I awoke with night sweats. I had been dreaming about Neal's old pair of scissors, the ones with the filigreed handles; the ones with the dull yet pointed tips. The ones I had left in my office desk drawer.

Almost fully awake, I realized that I wanted those scissors, though I had rarely used them, and even then, mainly to open the taped packages of books typically sent by publishers who wanted me to try their new composition handbook. Those scissors had rested comfortably in Neal's desk for years I couldn't count. They had been mine since I took over his office back in 2002. Mine, but now they and whatever else I had chosen to let lie in that office would be imploded in a few days as the building that housed us, the flagstone building of campus—Neville Hall—was scheduled for a complete renovation. Why did I think I could abandon those scissors? Even though I could live and work and completely function without them, why did I suddenly find them indispensible?

They could never save a life and they didn't even cut well.

So I drove to campus the next day, a 90-mile round trip—for the sole purpose of rescuing those scissors. My younger daughter Layla and a student I've mentored for the past two years, Erika, joined me as I toured my now almost vacant office for this heretofore unprecious item. They were where they always were—safe in that drawer—never knowing that they had almost gone the way of other useless items in that building. As far as we know, only the old outer bricks will remain, and I can only hope that whatever asbestos is left in the walls will not show up one day in other unwanted places. I say this, because three former dwellers of this revered building died of inoperable cancers, and who knows, really, what caused these terminal growths—growths that simply were too large and diffused to be cut out.

As I left my office for that final time, I stared at the VHS cassettes that I was leaving: *Rear Window, Raising Arizona*, Chaplin's shorts. I gazed at the round window, my only office window that

opened when you pushed it counter-clockwise. I gazed, too, at the
James Joyce poster that one of my colleagues demanded I take.
Joyce's odd and asymmetrical eyes stared at me for over twenty
years, but will no more. My Joyce image, after all, is only paper,
but scissors, now, they're rock-solid. So I placed them in the glove
compartment of my car where if I ever need them, I'll know where to
look.

*

Layla graduated last week, too, from the college where I've taught
English for the past twenty-nine years. 29, as we know, is a prime
number. That means nothing to this story, and during the two weeks
before Layla graduated, I wondered if my twenty-nine years meant
anything to the college.

We're a small, rural, liberal arts school, and in our promotional
literature, the papers and brochures sent out to prospective students, we quite often refer to ourselves as a "family." We should
always consider the deeper and wider implications of the words we
use.

For instance, I know a family that refuses to mention or have
mentioned their younger son's name. The gay son; the one who died
of AIDS. My own mother warned me when we visited them once:
Now don't mention Kevin. They don't speak about him."

Or the mother who sits shiva for her son when he marries a
woman outside of the faith, even though she herself, a self-diag-
nosed agoraphobic, never went to Temple. Or the couple that tells
their youngest daughter that they had her so that she could be the
"spare child," insurance in case one of her older siblings died, which,
of course, happened some fifty years later.

You know.

Family.

So, at our college, there is a tradition where at graduation,
parents may come to the dais and "assist" in the conferring of their
child's degree. It's a beautiful moment, one that surely happens
only at small colleges and maybe nowhere other than my own. A few
weeks before she graduated, Layla asked if I was going to help hand
her the coveted diploma.

"Of course, sweetie. I'd be honored."

I didn't tell her how deeply moved I was that this mattered to
her. Not always as academically motivated as I had hoped she would

be, Layla had nevertheless blossomed in her study of psychology, even making the Provost's List in her last year.

Pleased as I was, I walked into the Provost's office a day or two later and asked if we could make this happen. I assumed that all I had to do was tell them, that they would make a note somewhere in the Provost's list of graduates, and all would follow from there. But when I asked, what I noticed was some uncomfortable silence. The Provost looked at his aide who looked at the secretary, who looked back at the Provost.

"Let us check into this," our chief academic officer said.

"Well, OK, but all I want is to walk on the stage and hand Layla her diploma."

The way they were acting, I wondered whether they thought I wanted to make a few remarks, or bring other members of the family up to the dais, too. The looks on their faces said, "Uh-oh," but I couldn't see why. The whole affair would take a matter of seconds.

A few hours later, I received an email from our alumni director:

"We're very sorry to deny your request. This is the oldest and strongest rule on campus: parents who assist in graduation must be alums of the college."

One of the first things I did upon receiving this message was to check through the pages of the faculty by-laws. I found no such rule.

I then checked with the Provost, who told me that he had no such rule written anywhere in his office. I emailed our President who said he knew of the policy and that maybe it was time for a review, adding:

"But we won't be able to undertake such a review in time for this year's graduation. "

He said he hoped that this decision would not sour graduation for me or my family. My wife looked at me when I told her and said, "Well, this does us a lot of good."

Layla herself was disappointed, but in her typical way, she let it go. There were too many other things to enjoy or worry about before graduation.

I tried one last time, however. I emailed the alumni director asking if this really were a codified, written rule, or whether it was merely a tradition we follow. To my knowledge no one knows how long we've practiced this beautiful acknowledgment, or how it began. When the director wrote back, she tried to salve the wound by complimenting Layla profusely. And then she added,

"If we let you do this, then the gates would open and everyone would want to take the stage. We've already had to turn down requests. I'll try to put my finger on this rule and get back to you."

But she never did. Perhaps it's because she hasn't found the rule yet, written on that magic sheet of paper, the one that was to keep me from handing another sheet of (is it still sheepskin?) paper to my daughter. I like to think that I've never overinflated my sense of who I am. Twenty-nine years, though?

Graduation morning dawned sunny and relatively mild in our South Carolina home. I sat on the first row of faculty watching those we taught and sometimes loved march across the dais. About halfway through came Layla, and as the president handed her diploma to her, I choked up. A colleague patted me on the shoulder; another whispered, "Is that your daughter?"

"Yes, she's mine."

Before the ceremony began, however, another colleague, knowing what I couldn't do that day, suggested that after the event, Layla and I climb the dais and re-enact the conferring. Why hadn't I thought of this?

So on Facebook and in our collective phones, there are pictures of me handing Layla her folder containing both her BS in Psychology and an engraving of Neville Hall, my old building, which was the backdrop for the ceremony. There are pictures of me kissing and hugging my college graduate, too. No one else appears with us, but I don't see the dais as empty. What is empty are the gestures of those who believe that policies shouldn't change, who hide behind unwritten rules on papers they can't find, as if they are keeping something sacred. As if they are the gatekeepers for some form of honored family tradition.

As if the hurt they inflict in this process will ever heal.

*

Family is often more than you think it is or could be. Erika graduated with Layla because, of course, they started college together. They didn't know each other back then, though I knew both of them. I had been on the committee that awarded Erika our highest scholarship—a full ride, books and all. I'll never forget our interview with Erika, or the evening before when I met her and her parents for the first time at a dinner for all scholarship finalists. After the meal, Erika's mother asked me if I had any advice for Erika, whose interviews would be the following today.

"Just be yourself," I said, which sounds like such a cliché, except that after speaking with this eighteen-year old young woman for even an hour, I knew there was a maturity, a deep wisdom about her. I remember her mother's reaction after Erika won the scholarship: "That was exactly what she needed to hear!"

I knew I didn't really know this family, but knowing and feeling so very often don't mate well.

It so happened that Layla and Erika joined the same sorority during their first semester, and you'd think such a move, particularly on a small campus, would ensure their becoming close friends. But that didn't happen. I don't pretend to understand all the reasons why they didn't. Of course, friendships can't be bought, nor can you ensure that all family members will get along. I asked Layla once if she was friends with Erika,

"She's a sweet girl," Layla answered, "but we're really different."

I know better than to ask my daughter to expound on such feelings, and I didn't know Erika well enough to comment, much less to ask her what she thought of Layla. Though this too is a cliché and a distortion of both young women, it's like they were the sisters in *Modern Family*, Hayley and Alex. Certain types, you know, except that when examined more closely, you can see that even TV characters are more rounded and complex than as seen on first viewing, or even after several years.

So I'll take credit for extending this family. I had been working so hard with Erika to develop her creative nonfiction, so I invited her and two other creative writing students to a family supper one Sunday night this past spring.

I asked Layla to join us, which she was glad to do. She wanted to come by herself, though (our home is 45 miles from the college), because, in her words, "It's too awkward since I don't know them that well." That night I cooked Layla's favorite supper—grillades and cheese grits—and our gathering went on well past 10:00. No one wanted to leave even though we were all tired. Or maybe it was the late night coffee complementing the fresh fruit and gelato. In any case, the next time I saw both Layla and Erika, they said as one even though their remarks came hours apart,

"I wish I had gotten to know Layla/Erika better, before now, now that we are almost ready to leave."

When my older daughter, Pari, met Erika a few weeks later, she claimed this new friend as the "third Barr daughter."

"Can't we adopt her," Pari asked my wife and me?

"Well we could," my wife said, "except that I don't think Erika is up for adoption."

Still, you know family when you meet them.

Erika gave the graduation speech, her privilege as outstanding senior. In that speech she told the story of standing on a mountaintop at the home of her best friend's grandmother. It's a place she can always come back to, she said, except that from now on her best friend won't be with her. Such is the reality of graduating and moving on. Of leaving a place you've called home for those four life-changing years. Her words touched me, and I felt them even more strongly as Layla walked across the stage. I thought too of Pari's mountain home in western Virginia, of all the leaving my wife and I have experienced. When Pari graduated from Wofford College, I wondered if I could ever go back there, to the city of Spartanburg, again. The paradox, a term Erika used so successfully about her sense of place in that speech, is that I have to go to Spartanburg because my therapist works in that town. To get therapy, I must walk through my fear of the ghosts of my joy.

I did get through those ghosts, partly because I wrote my way through them: pages and pages of life ghosts that became my first book. Writing about family allows that family to understand, to wince a little, and to grow. One day I came home to find a package waiting on me: my book, with a handwritten note on a yellowed piece of paper. A note from Pari's boyfriend's Dad. He loved the book and realized that our boyhoods and family stories—his in Virginia, mine in Alabama—followed similar emotional journeys. "Would you sign my copy and send it back," Bill Baker asked. Of course I will, Bill. Of course.

During graduation day I also was suffering from some sort of sinus cold. So I could blame my widespread Kleenex use on that, as Layla got her degree without my assistance. Though bitter, that bitterness, as our President hoped, did not erase my joy. As Layla and I stood on the dais after everyone else had pretty much headed on to lunch celebrations, I looked out onto the area just below the dais. There was our family, Erika's family, and Layla's boyfriend Billy's family—all watching us, all smiling at us, and I saw my own joy reflected in them. Neville Hall was still behind us in the form that I've always known it, and everyone made those pictures of us that are more than digital paper. That afternoon at a barbecue hosted by Layla and her housemates, Billy's father toasted us with an excellent and very dry Chardon. Later that night his mother texted us as they drove back to Charleston:

"I miss my new family," her text said.

I know what she means.

I don't always remember my dreams, and usually when I do, I report them to my wife who helps me try to interpret them. Often, she offers the interpretation for me, but even when she does, she adds this caveat:

The meaning is up to you, of course. It's your choice."

From the dais where I ended that ceremony, I looked out on the campus plaza. There was so much to remember: past graduations where once I gave the commencement speech, my papers rustling through my nervousness. To see: the stone building across Broad Street where my office will lie next year. But I chose this scene: a space that Layla and Erika and I had visited on the day we rescued my scissors. A space we visited together only *because* I dreamed about those scissors.

A green space encasing rows of bricks.

Each senior class has the option of buying their own personalized brick, inscribed with whatever they want to say. The three of us visited these latest bricks just after lunch at Yo Cup (featuring Red Rooster coffee from the mountains of Floyd, Virginia). The girls were excited to see their names, the $75 bricks that would place them permanently at the college campus they loved. The bricks are arranged by the maintenance crew in whatever order the crew determines. So the three of us stood looking for these two bricks, noticing the ones that had misspellings and the ones featuring students who weren't quite ready to move on yet.

And then we found theirs: Layla Adele Barr, Erika Laine Gotfredson.

Side by side.

"See, you guys were always meant to be together," I stated with all obviousness.

"That's so cool," they both said, and all I could do was wonder at the pairing, the beautiful juxtaposition of these two adults who lived parallel campus lives for their four undergraduate years.

We know that bricks don't last forever, and that we can't remember all the precious moments in our lives. But we do make choices, sometimes thinking through them, sometimes not:

One, two, three, *shoot*.

What these choices have revealed is that through cutting and pasting seemingly unconnected objects and people; by engraving precious letters in the thickness of brick and setting them next to each other, what isn't exactly gold, but *golden*, will stay. Will outlast any strong rule, or strict policy, or even any dear but murky tradition.

For these letters *are* the glowing images I see, appearing before me in the spaces of my memory, in the words that come to me from somewhere in the middle of my night.

Jorge Luis Borges

Pierre Menard, the Author of Don Quixote

translated by Norman Thomas Di Giovanni
text from Project Gutenburg

to Silvina Ocampo

The *visible* body of work left by the novelist Pierre Menard is easily and briefly listed. Inexcusable, therefore, are the omissions and additions perpe-trated by Madame Henri Bachelier in a misleading check—list which a certain newspaper that makes no secret of its Protestant leanings has had the insensitivity to thrust upon its unfortunate readers—few and Calvinist though these be, when not Freemason or circumcised. Menard's true friends looked on this checklist with alarm and even a certain sadness. Only yesterday, in a manner of speaking, did we gather among the mournful cypresses at his final resting place, and already Error creeps in to blur his Mem—ory. Unquestionably, some small rectification is in order.

It is all too easy, I realize, to challenge my meagre credentials. Nevertheless, I trust that I shall not be disallowed from citing the names of two eminent patrons. The Baroness of Bacourt (at whose unforgettable vendredis it was my privilege to come to know the late-lamented poet) has been kind enough to grant approval to the pages that follow. The Countess of Bagnoreggio, one of the most refined minds of the Principality of Monaco (now of Pittsburgh, Pennsylvania, following her recent marriage to the international philanthropist Simon Kautzsch, a man much vilified, alas, by the victims of his disinterested activities), has sacri—ficed 'to truth and to the death' (her own words) the aristocratic reserve that so distinguishes her, and in an open letter published in the review Luxe she too grants me her approbation. These patents, I believe, should suffice.

I have said that Menard's visible work is readily listed. After careful examination of his private papers, I find that they contain the following items:

A Symbolist sonnet which appeared twice (the sec—ond time

with variants) in the review *La Conque* (March and October, 1899).

A study of the feasibility of constructing a poetic vocabulary of concepts that are neither synonyms for nor circumlocutions of those that shape our everyday speech 'but ideal objects created by consensus and intended essentially for poetic needs' (Nîmes, 1901).

A study of 'certain connections or affinities' in the thinking of Descartes, Leibniz, and John Wilkins (Nîmes, 1903).

A study of Leibniz's *Characteristica Universalis* (Nîmes, 1904).

A technical article on the possibility of enriching the game of chess by removing one of the rook's pawns. Menard sets forth his case, elaborates, argues, and in the end rejects his own innovation.

A study of Ramon Lull's *Ars Magna Generalis* (Nîmes, 1906).

A translation, with a foreword and notes, of *The Book of the Free Invention and Art of the Game of Chess* by Ruy López de Segura (Paris, 1907).

The draft pages of a monograph on George Boole's symbolic logic.

An examination of the basic metrical laws of French prose, illustrated with examples from Saint-Simon (*Revue des langues romanes*, Montpellier, October, 1909).

A reply to Luc Durtain (who had denied the existence of such laws), illustrated with examples from Luc Durtain (*Revue des langues romanes*, Montpellier, December, 1909).

A manuscript translation of Quevedo's *Aguja de navegar cultos*, entitled *La boussole des précieux.*

A foreword to the catalogue of an exhibition of litho—graphs by Carolus Hourcade (Nîmes, 1914).

Problems with a Problem (Paris, 1917), a book discuss—ing in chronological order the solutions to the well-known paradox of Achilles and the tortoise. To date, two editions of this book have appeared; the second bears in an epi—graph Leibniz's advice, 'Have not the slightest fear, Mr Tortoise', and amends the chapters on Russell and Descartes.

A dogged analysis of Toulet's 'syntactic usage' (*Nouvelle Revue Française*, March, 1921). Menard, I recall, held that censure and praise are sentimental activities which have little or nothing to do with criticism.

A transposition into alexandrines of Paul Valéry's 'Cimitière marin' (*N.R.F.*, January, 1928).

An invective against Paul Valéry in Jacques Reboul's *Pages Towards the Suppression of Reality.* (This denunciation, if I may digress, is the exact reverse of his true opinion of Valéry. Valéry knew this, and the old friendship between the two men was not imperilled.)

A 'definition' of the Countess of Bagnoreggio, in—cluded in the 'triumphant tome'—the words of another contributor, Gabriele D'Annunzio—published annually by this lady for the purpose of correcting the inevitable false—hoods of the gutter press and of presenting 'to the world and to Italy' a true portrait of her person, so often exposed (by reason of her beauty and conduct) to over-hasty misinterpretation.

An admirable crown of sonnets for the Baroness of Bacourt (1934).

A handwritten list of verses whose effect derives from their punctuation.*

The above, then, is a summary in chronological order (omitting only a few woolly occasional sonnets inscribed in Madame Henri Bachelier's hospitable, or greedy, album) of Menard's *visible* work. I shall now move on to his other work—the underground, the infinitely heroic, the singular, and (oh, the scope of the man!) the unfinished. This oeuvre, possibly the most significant of our time, consists of chapters nine and thirty-eight of the first part of *Don Quixote* and of a fragment of chapter twenty-two. I am aware that my claim will seem an absurdity, but to vindicate this 'absurdity' is the principle object of the present essay.**

Two texts of differing value inspired Menard's under—taking. One was that philological fragment (number 2005 in the Dresden edition) in which Novalis outlines the notion of *total* identification with a particular author. The other was one of those derivative books that place Christ on a boulevard, Hamlet in the Cannebière, or Don Quixote on Wall Street. Like any man of good taste, Menard loathed such pointless masquerades, since all they were fit for, he said, was to amuse the man in the street with anachronisms or, worse still, to bewitch us with the infantile idea that every

---

*Madame Henri Bachelier also lists a literal translation of Quevedo's literal translation of St Francis of Sales's *Introduction à la vie dévote*. No trace of this work is to be found in Pierre Menard's li—brary. The ascription must have arisen from something our friend said in jest, which the lady misunderstood.

**I had a secondary purpose as well—to sketch a portrait of Pierre Menard. But dare I compete with the gilded pages that I am told the Baroness of Bacourt is preparing, or with Carolus Hourcade's delicate, precise pencil?

historical period is the same or is different. What seemed to Menard
more interesting—albeit superficial and inconsistent in execution—
was Daudet's famous attempt to combine in *one* character, Tartarin,
both the Ingenious Knight and his squire. Anyone who suggests that
Menard dedicated his life to writing a modern-day *Don Quixote* de-
files Menard's living memory.

Pierre Menard was not out to write another *Don Quixote*—which
would have been easy—but *Don Quixote itself.* Needless to add, he
never envisaged a mindless transcription of the original; it was not
his intention to copy it. His ambition, an admirable one, was to pro-
duce a handful of pages that matched word for word and line for line
those of Miguel de Cervantes.

'Only my aim is astonishing,' he wrote to me from Bayonne on
the thirtieth of September 1934. 'The final term, the conclusion, of
a theological or metaphysical proof—about, say, the objective world,
God, causation, platonic forms—is just as foregone and familiar as
my well-known novel. The one difference is that the philosopher
gives us in pretty volumes the intermediary stages of his work,
while I have chosen to destroy mine.' In fact, not a single draft page
remains to bear witness to Menard's many years of toil.

The first method he devised was relatively simple. To learn
Spanish well, to return to the Catholic faith, to fight the Moor and
Turk, to forget European history from 1602 to 1918, to be Miguel
de Cervantes. This was the course Pierre Menard embarked upon
(I know he gained a fair command of seventeenth-century Spanish), but he rejected the method as too easy. Too impossible, rather!
the reader will say. Granted, but the scheme was impossible from
the start, and of all the impossible ways of achieving his aim this
was the least interesting. To be in the twentieth century a popular
novelist of the seventeenth century seemed to him a belittlement.
To be, however possible, Cervantes and to come to *Don Quixote*
seemed less exacting—therefore less interesting—than to stay
Pierre Menard and come to *Don Quixote* through the experience
of Pierre Menard. (This conviction, let me add, made him leave out
the autobiographical prologue to the second part of *Don Quixote.*
To have retained this prologue would have been to create another
character—Cervantes—and would also have meant presenting *Don
Quixote* through this character and not through Menard. Naturally,

Menard denied himself this easy way out.) 'In essence, my scheme is
not difficult,' I read in another part of his letter. 'To carry it through
all I need is to be immortal.' Should I confess that I often find myself
thinking that he finished the book and that I read *Don Quixote*—all of
Don Quixote—as if it had been Menard's brainchild? A few nights ago,
leafing through chapter twenty-six, which he never tried his hand
at, I recognized our friend's style and voice in this fine phrase: 'the
nymphs of the streams, the damp and doleful Echo...' This effective
coupling of a moral and a physical adjective brought back to me a line
of Shakespeare's that Menard and I talked about one evening: Where
a malignant and a turbaned Turk...

But why *Don Quixote*? our reader will ask. For a Spaniard such a
choice would have been understandable; not, however, for a Symbolist poet from Nîmes, an ardent follower of Poe, who begat Baude-
laire, who begat Valéry, who begat Edmond Teste. The letter quoted
above sheds light on the point. '*Don Quixote*,' explains Menard, 'inter-
ests me deeply but does not seem to me—how can I put it?—inevitable. While I find it hard to imagine a world without Edgar Allan Poe's
interjection,

Ah, bear in mind this garden was enchanted!

or without the "Bateau ivre" or the "Ancient Mariner," I am quite
able to imagine it without *Don Quixote*. (Of course, I am talking
about my own ability and not about the historical resonance of these
works.) *Don Quixote* is an incidental book; *Don Quixote* is not necessary. I
can therefore plan the writing of it—I can write it—without the risk of
tautology. I read it from cover to cover when I was about twelve or
thirteen. Since then, I have carefully reread certain chapters—those
that for the moment I shall not try my hand at. I have also delved
into Cervantes's one-act farces, his comedies, *Galatea*, the exem-
plary novels, the all-too laboured *Travails of Persiles and Segismunda*,
and the *Voyage to Parnassus*. My overall recollection of *Don Quixote*,
simplified by forgetfulness and lack of interest, is much like the hazy
outline of a book one has before writing it. Given this outline (which
can hardly be denied me), it goes without saying that my problem
is somewhat more difficult than the one Cervantes faced. My oblig-

ing forerunner, far from eschewing the collaboration of chance, went about writing his immortal work in something of a devil-may-care spirit, carried along by the inertial force of language and invention. I have taken upon myself the mysterious duty of reconstructing his spontaneous novel word for word. My solitary game is governed by two contradictory rules. The first allows me to try out variations of a formal or psychological nature; the second makes me sacrifice these variations to the "original" text while finding solid reasons for doing so. To these assumed obstacles we must add another—an in-built one. To compose *Don Quixote* at the beginning of the seventeenth century was reasonable, necessary, and perhaps even predestined; at the beginning of the twentieth century, however, it is well-nigh impossible. Three centuries, packed with complex events, have not passed without effect. One of these events was *Don Quixote* itself.

In spite of this trio of obstacles, Menard's fragmentary *Don Quixote* is subtler than that of Cervantes. Cervantes sets up a crude contrast between the fantasy of the chivalric tale and the tawdry reality of the rural Spain he knew, whereas Menard chooses as his reality the land of Carmen during the century of Lepanto and Lope de Vega. What picturesque touches would this not have suggested to a Maurice Barrès or a Dr. Rodríguez Larreta! Menard, with complete unselfconsciousness, avoids the least hint of exoticism. We find in his work no gypsydom, no conquistadores, no mystics, no Philip II, no burnings at the stake. He does away with local colour. This disdain hints at a new treatment of the historical novel. This disdain is an outright condemnation of *Salammbô*.

If we examine isolated chapters we are equally astonished. Let us, for example, look into chapter thirty-eight of part one, 'in which don Quixote gives a strange discourse on arms and letters.' We all know that don Quixote (like Quevedo in an analogous later passage from his *Hora de todos*) finds for arms over letters. Cervantes was an old soldier; his finding is understandable. But that the don Quixote of Pierre Menard, a contemporary of *La trahison des clercs* and of Bertrand Russell, should relapse into such fuzzy sophistry! Madame Bachelier sees this as the author subordinating himself in an admirable and characteristic way to the mentality of his hero; others, showing not the slightest perceptiveness, see only a *tran-*

scription of Don Quixote; the Baroness of Bacourt sees the influence
of Nietzsche. To this third view (which I consider beyond dispute) I
wonder if I dare add a fourth, which accords quite well with Pierre
Menard's all but divine modesty—his self—effacing or ironic habit
of propagating ideas that were the exact reverse of those he himself
held. (Let us once more remember his diatribe against Paul Valéry
in Jacques Reboul's short-lived super-realist pages.) Cervantes's
text and Menard's are identical as to their words, but the second is
almost infinitely richer. (More ambiguous, his detractors will claim,
but the ambiguity is itself a richness.)

It is a revelation to compare Menard's *Don Quixote* with Cervantes's. The latter, for example, wrote (part one, chapter nine):

> *...truth, whose mother is history, rival of time, storehouse of
> great deeds, witness to the past, example and admonition to the
> present, warning to the future.*

Written in the seventeenth century, written by the 'lay genius' Cervantes, this catalogue is no more than a rhetorical eulogy to history.
Menard, on the other hand, writes:

> *...truth, whose mother is history, rival of time, storehouse of great
> deeds, witness to the past, example and admonition to the present,
> warning to the future.*

History, the 'mother' of truth; the idea is breathtaking. Menard,
the contemporary of William James, does not define history as an
enquiry into reality but as its source. To him historic truth is not
what actually took place, it is what we think took place. The last two
phrases—'example and admonition to the present, warning to the
future'—are shamelessly pragmatic.

As vivid is the contrast in styles. Menard's, deliberately archaic—
he was a foreigner, after all—is prone to certain affectations. Not so
the style of his forerunner, who uses the everyday Spanish of his time
with ease.

There is no intellectual exercise which in the end is not pointless. A philosophical tenet is at the outset a true description of the
world; with the passage of time it becomes no more than a chapter—perhaps only a paragraph or a name—in the history of

philosophy. In literature this eventual withering away is even plain-
er. *Don Quixote*, Menard once told me, was first and foremost an
entertaining book; now it has become a pretext for patriotic toasts,
grammatical arrogance, and obscene deluxe editions. Fame is a form
of incomprehension—perhaps the worst.

There is nothing new in such nihilistic conclusions; what is
unusual is the resolve that Pierre Menard derived from them. Determined to rise above the emptiness that awaits all man's endeavours,
he embarked upon a task that was extremely complex and, even
before it began, futile. He devoted his utmost care and attention to
reproducing, in a language not his own, a book that already exist-
ed. He wrote draft after draft, revising assiduously and tearing up
thousands of manuscript pages.*** He never let anyone see them and
took pains to ensure they did not survive him. I have tried without
success to reconstruct them.

It seems to me that the 'final' *Don Quixote* can be looked on as a
kind of palimpsest in which traces—faint but still decipherable—of
our friend's 'earlier' writing must surely shine through. Unfortu-
nately, only a second Pierre Menard, working his way back over the
pages of the first one, would be capable of digging up and restoring
to life those lost Troys.

'To think, to analyse, to invent,' Menard also wrote to me, 'far
from being exceptional acts are the way the intelligence breathes.
To glorify one particular instance of this action, to store as treasure
the ancient thoughts of others, to recollect in amazed disbelief what
the *doctor universalis* thought is to admit to our own indolence and
crudeness. Every man should be capable of all ideas, and I believe that
in the future he will.'

Through a new technique, using deliberate anachronisms and
false attributions, Menard (perhaps without trying to) has enriched
the static, fledgling art of reading.

Infinite in its possibilities, this technique prompts us to reread the *Odyssey* as if it came after the *Aeneid* and Ma—dame Henri

---

***I remember his notebooks with their square-ruled pages, the heavy black
deletions, the personal system of symbols he used for marginal emendations, and his
minute handwriting. He liked to stroll through the outskirts of Nîmes at sunset, often
taking along a notebook with which he would make a cheerful bonfire.

Bachelier's book *The Centaur's Garden* as if it were written by Madame Henri Bachelier. The technique fills the mildest of books with adventure. To attribute *The Imitation of Christ* to Louis Ferdinand Céline or to James Joyce—would this not be a satisfactory renewal of its subtle spiritual lessons?

Nîmes, 1939

Ashley Chambers

from The Exquisite Buoyancies: A Sonography

Little little   Here here   Little hither   Here little
                              hangs
                                        my trunked habit of 1 halted Gold
spilling yr crested Shall —

Ashley Chambers

from The Exquisite Buoyancies: A Sonography

                                        Little touch w out looking Baby
                        touch

w out breathing   another deflated decoy
                                                        boohoo
                                        -ing, a retarded
lamb mooing wildwide   eweless & baaless for body-body
                                        but not You
                        baby   still not You—

Ashley Chambers

from The Exquisite Buoyancies: A Sonography

Little Just   just 1 more sputtering snare but not you baby   until I sun
-silence my own cackle my own cluck or   the Die Oftener   until I white-
                                                      light What
I won't w out yr Secretswept Sacrament of the not Earth scarce
-ly advising a Fatalspeeching a Foundbeneather a Phonyluminous to stun
-bright You baby   prostrating   my benumbed oncepink,   the plush
cradle white but ascending still for Who but
                                        You   Born to
                              consume the Event Born
          again   if only
                              to depart again

                  No, Live   not into an Again   but

          A Live, You Little

Vindicated   Ruddy   Adroit
                                        Live

                              Baby, Live —

Ashley Chambers

from The Exquisite Buoyancies: A Sonography

Live my reorganize of seed   & some other angels maybe   The Unvoiced
        If Ever God forbade me to render in perennial bloods
Yes   Little   Manifest   Martian   my manifest bloods ravenous
bloods w voice ajar yes & the bulk the bulk
                                        of yr body-body   also song
is the white parts mating still —

Ashley Chambers

from The Exquisite Buoyancies: A Sonography

A climb of grief I weep-wade to examine yr gums laid bare like blessing
            in gorgeous permission my Alien Power embers yr soft
skull

        in Unthreatening Gesture
        in placement of Celestial Diadem
        in Loud Snap

                                You are   the More Song
You White Little Fox —

Ashley Chambers

from The Exquisite Buoyancies: A Sonography

The white parts echo again the white parts to make me crazy the white parts
who go running the white parts keeping busy w the tremendous white parts
Who Rise Up against the white parts I bury yr nose the cocoon white the
mouth white & awash w white I iron yr brows against the white piers echo
again I press yr wet mouth into my white wet palm yr tongue floundering
to snake against the white parts yr tongue against my white wet palm goes
running makes me crazy the white cradle running to make me crazy
the white parts mating weep-wading to examine my blessing My Baby
You Gorgeous My Alien White My Alien Parts go running You go running You
must go running Baby you must—

Ashley Chambers

from The Exquisite Buoyancies: A Sonography

This uneaten everlasting silk is yr skin & my milk   songs ecstatic
white Hands   Who   Burn   to contract yr death is now a story
I can report

        w   my   Gold —

Sheldon Lee Compton

Beautiful

Mom is dead in the living room. She could have been beautiful, but she was stubborn. She could never understand human preference, how it could change over time, become something else, white instead of black, black instead of white. My uncles said she inherited such crippling stubbornness from my grandfather, who lived just long enough to see arms and legs become ugly.

Mom's oldest brother, Royal, may have gotten his fair share, too. Royal sits across from the closed casket. Anybody nearby can hear him muttering how stupid it was, having a closed casket for a woman who died of perfectly natural causes. He was the first amputee in our family, but not by choice.

Royal lost his arm in Afghanistan at just the right time, when local college students were just starting to clip off their fingers at the first joint. Royal came home and was an immediate celebrity around the high school. He took a job as a maintenance guy, and the kids would not leave him alone. They wanted to know what it felt like. Was there really such a thing as a phantom limb? At least ten times a day a student would ask him to unpin the fold of his shirt sleeve so they could see the smooth stub. He finally told us about it when a female student asked him to hang out with her after school.

It seemed the high school students were just catching on to the shift. Some had friends in college who had already cut their fingers as far up as the second joint. One young man clipped the fingers and thumb of his left hand in this way. It occurred to Royal the students at his school were screwing up their courage by questioning him.

The first at the high school to take a finger was the girl who asked Royal to hang out. Melody Masters. The front office sent him to the cafeteria to replace a fluorescent first thing that morning. When he stepped through to the main lunch hall, his half-ladder wedged beneath his good arm, he saw Melody standing in the middle of the room. A group of no less than twenty students surrounded her. She had her hand out in front of her. Her index finger was wrapped in gauze and needed changing. It was maroon-splotched with dried blood.

It took little time for news to spread to the administration, and the next morning a student body meeting was called across the intercom. Students, teachers, and staff piled into the gym to find Principal Akers standing with Melody at a podium mid-court. The message was clear. Behavior such as that exhibited by Miss Masters was a clear sign of a mental and emotional distress, whether brought on by a medical condition or as a product of basic peer pressure.

Principal Akers motioned to the young girl's parents sitting court side, naming them as brave and caring individuals willing to attend the emergency meeting to stand together against such unbelievable and atrocious activities.

None of it worked. The movement against what came to be known as clipping went statewide with legislators introducing bills to first combat and then outlaw what they called the most extreme body modification imaginable. None of it mattered. Clipping continued, and soon became outright amputating. If missing a finger was attractive, a missing arm, a missing leg, was beautiful.

Royal quit his job after the number of students with missing arms soared to more than twenty. He stayed home most all the time, taking his veteran's pension and keeping the curtains drawn. There was a lot to be missed, and he was happy to do so.

Years passed and human preference turned from white to black, from one set of agreements to another, as gradually as it must have been for the world to agree that a clear sky was the color blue. As with anything else, there were extremes. Some could only stomach lopping off the top or bottom of an ear, mostly business professionals, while others went full quad, depending forevermore on the kindness of those who very nearly worshiped us FQs as gods and goddesses.

By the time Mom died, she was one of only three in our town of more than six-thousand residents who tragically had not fallen in line. Royal eventually came to be thought of as one of the other two. The third person no one knew, but had only heard about in conversation.

When visitors start crowding the room, Royal heads to the porch. He stays there while they all take turns walking to the casket and tapping it or laying their hands across the top, shaking their heads, dry-eyed. After most of them have gone, he comes back into the living room and works his fingers under the casket lid, opens it slowly.

A couple cousins make moves to stop him, but I call them off with a shake of my head. It's a pitiful site, but it's his to see. He can stare as long as he likes.

Jack Harvey

A Valediction Forbidding Whoring

Cut the foreplay
out of your heart,
young Lochinvar, Lothario, Lothar
whoever you are;
the art of life
's serious business;
more than a buss on the kisser.

Pass quickly the primrose path;
there's no time for fooling,
you fool,
there's no time for sporting
or spinning
on Ferris wheels

like crazy.

Pass quickly the
turbulent flesh-press;
this race is not
to the timely tortoise
dragging his carapace,
or the braggart hare.

Come to;
be specific in the Pacific,
vast blue sink
sunk in the middle of nowhere.
Ready or not,
here you go,
the strangling seawater
forcing your gullet
while your twining hair

follows its spiral,
following you,
falling,
slow as sand,
into the crushing dark.

Deep in the final hole
and upcoming in the
finial heaven
it's God himself gapes
through singing whales;
breaching
heights above heights,
giants pile Pelions
on a wart.

The King of the Sea is
a red herring, they say,
and leaves no trace as he swims;
the burning bush ends up
burned to ashes
in the fireplace.

Prodigal as the desert sheiks
we end up
like old Valentino;
our cupboard
bare as a bone.

But let it go,
take heart Gregorio,
Orontes, not so young,
so glissando;
however hard the winter,
however scant the spring,
take your heart out
and eat it alive;
red-hot cannibal of love
merging love and prey,

lie and lay,
into one refined grey,
you can be

forever and a day.

Monica Hileman

Until We Get Ourselves Back

The last train had passed through the station and we waited at the fence for the guy to lock up and go home. Marcus knew where you could move a chunk of cement and squeeze under. "Look out for the third rail," said Kenny. He hoisted himself up onto the platform. Marcus gave me a boost. They jimmied the door, and we got inside the booth, only to find the heater didn't work.

"At least there's no wind," said Marcus.

We put down a layer of bus schedules, the station renovation notices, and a flattened box on the floor in the corner and sat squeezed together, our legs covered with sections of yesterday's Globe.

Kenny kept shifting around trying to get comfortable.

"No, don't get up." Right away I could feel the cold on that side and pressed closer to Marcus. The flimsy door banged shut and we could hear him taking a leak, so easy. Every time I drank something, I had to consider where we'd be later on.

"Hey," said Kenny. "There's a window open up there."

"Up where?" said Marcus. He made a move to get up.

Across from the platform stood a brick warehouse. We stared up at the window left open a few inches. It beckoned, it promised. Three stories up, it challenged us.

"I got an idea," said Marcus. He retrieved the chair from the booth. It was aluminum, easy to carry. Down across the tracks, we tossed it over the fence and squeezed under, the way we'd come in.

His idea was for me to sit on his shoulders: that way I would be able to reach up with the chair and hook the seat onto the bottom step of the fire escape. I got a good grip on the two back legs and stretched out my arms. "Go forward," said Kenny. After a couple tries I made contact and held on tight. The three of us pulling, we were able to lower it down and climb on. They were shouting and laughing as they clambered up behind me, so I told them to hush. There were houses on the next block and you could see us in the light from the tracks. The windows were tall, wood frame, each set in an arch of brickwork. To reach the one that was open somebody would have to slowly inch his way out along a narrow ledge.

"Why couldn't this one be open," said Kenny, meaning the window right in front of us.

"Try it," said Marcus.

Kenny took out the box cutter he carried, stuck it in the sash and when he tugged, it opened.

From the light shining in we could see the size of the room. It was big and nearly empty. We climbed in, and Marcus pulled the string on the dangling bulb. We saw the random furniture, and the canvases propped against the wall, some of them four feet high, covered with abstract smears of paint. But what really got our attention was the space heater. We switched it on and watched its two long bands turning red.

Only one door, no bathroom or even a closet: nobody lived here. Over in the corner was a sink. The water came out frigid at first. I got the temperature just right and let the liquid warmth pour over my hands. I washed my face, scooping it up again and again.

"How do you know it's any good if you don't know what it's 'sposed to be?" Marcus was saying.

"You feel it," said Kenny. They were standing in front of the paintings. "Or you don't. Like if somebody is telling you something, either you believe what they're saying or it doesn't add up." They moved on to another gloomy clash of green and black.

Marcus said, "What about this one?"

Kenny took a moment to answer. "I don't know if I want to feel that." He turned away, his face pulled to one side. "I mean, I already feel like that."

Marcus came over to the kitchen area where I was drying off with a stiff hand towel I found by the sink. "My grandma had one of these," he said, opening the breadbox. He took out a bagel in a plastic bag and tapped it on the countertop. "Hard as wood."

In the little fridge I found a half quart of milk. "Pew." The date on the carton was from a couple weeks ago.

Marcus held up a stack of mail. "Looks like somebody's away." He flipped through several addressed to "Occupant" before he came to an envelope with a name. "Mik-ha-il Pav-lovich."

At the desk, Kenny rifled thought the drawers. "Hey, hey. Look what I found." He held up a ring of keys, went to the door, and pulled it open to try each until he found the one that fit the lock and turned.

"What do you say we take a tour," said Marcus.

The hallways were long and wide with creaky wood floors, one side bare brick, the other a plaster wall painted with different scenes. Tropical fish. Giant grasshoppers. A field of poppies. All the doors to the studios had names and postcards showing samples of each artists' work. I made a beeline for the door that had only a drawing of a toilet.

The bug eyes of a caterpillar stared at us coming down the stairs onto the second floor landing, the rest of the fuzzy green body curved into the hallway where a jungle scene must have taken a bunch of people hours to paint, all those leaves and tangled vines.

We went down the back stairs to the first floor, past the wood-working shop that made a style of furniture partly fashioned from tree branches.

"Oh shit," said Kenny, seeing the metal box on the wall by the front entrance.

"Maybe only the doors and windows on the first floor are alarmed," said Marcus.

"But it's not lit up," I said. The panel was blank.

"It's not on," said Kenny.

"Maybe it's broke," said Marcus.

The front door had a metal grate covering the window. Kenny peeked out before he turned the bolt and pulled it open to find the key that worked. "This one must be the mailbox." He went and opened it. "Empty."

"Let's check out the roof," said Marcus on our way back up.

The fourth floor mural featured ocean waves and colorful birds in palm trees. At the end of the hall, a narrow stairs led up to a door barred with a plank. The steps were steep and unlit, so we were waiting in the dark for Marcus to get it open. I heard the scrape of wood, felt the rush of air and didn't want to go back into that cold, but there was Kenny behind me, so I stepped out onto the roof.

"Pretty close," said Marcus, gauging the distance between our building and the next. Kenny stepped back several feet for a running start and I almost yelled at him, afraid for a second that he really was going to jump across. Such a goof. From his sisters I'd heard how he used to drive them nuts when they were kids.

I turned toward Boston and saw the pink neon sign on the old Schrafft factory that I used to pass on my way to Julian's, the chi-chi restaurant where Kenny and I met. He made sauces and prepped orders. I waited tables. It was a good place to work while Silvio was in charge. Then his son took it over and one day called us all together to say that the lease was up and rather than pay the rent increase, we'd be moving. That's what he said. We knew different when some guys came around appraising the equipment. A month later we closed.

My apartment was bigger, so Kenny moved in with me. I found a job through a temp agency, then he did too, doing construction, but that soon dried up. When it came time to pay rent, we balked at using up what we had in the bank. I was against him selling his car, but it needed a brake job and a new exhaust. "And the tickets," said Kenny. "Better sell it now before they come and boot it."

We had enough to cover groceries and rent for April and May, but not June. Kenny's sister took us in, which was fine, until her asshole of a husband came back and Kenny, who can get along with anyone, got into a fight with him, and we ended up spending half the night in Dunkin Donuts. Friends put us up; in their living room, on a screened-in porch, in a tent pitched in the backyard.

I wasn't discouraged because we were both working again. Kenny had a job for a couple weeks taking down the remnants of a burnt-out building, and I happened upon a new bistro in the South End. I talked to the owner who said to come in tomorrow and report to Candace, the manager.

Candace expected to put together her own staff and didn't appreciate him hiring me—that's how it felt when I went in the next day. Things got off to a bad start and my second week on the job she cornered me in the supply room to ask, "Shouldn't you have ironed that blouse?"

I thought maybe she'd understand if she knew my circumstances, which wouldn't last much longer because with the money Kenny and I were saving, soon we'd have our own place.

I saw the tightening in her jaw, the slight shift of her body away from me. "What was that address you put on the application?" I'd put my old address. I had to put something. She accused me of lying and said I had no right to be working in a restaurant dealing with the public.

Get a job. How many times had I thought that when a panhandler asked me for money? Well, panhandling is a job. It requires a set of skills, like any other. Kenny and I were too dispirited to be stopping people with a story about getting into a jam and needing subway fare, or a few bucks for a ticket back home, or whatever; we were begging, pure and simple. Either you made it seem like they could be part of the solution by chipping in to send you on your way, or you let them see the strain edging on despair so they would think, There but for the grace of God go I and reach into their pocket to give you a portion of what they might contribute to their favorite charity. Kenny made a sign that said, "Give direct. 100% to needy recipients."

I was afraid someone I knew would see me there on the sidewalk. Kids stared. "Mommy, why's that lady there?" What lady? the mother might have said. She'd looked right through me both times they passed. I'd been worried what people would think, as if anybody cared. After a while I longed for someone who did know me (or knew me) to come along—someone who would appreciate what it meant for me to be standing there. College graduate, I would have put on my sign, if I'd made one.

Kenny had the idea to borrow his sister's guitar. He sounded as good as a guy we heard singing on the platform at Park Street. A fiddler said we'd have to get a license, but maybe that was to play in the subway. Kenny figured he'd serenade the office workers at lunchtime along the path between the hill and the bandstand on The Common.

People walked by, a few stopped to listen. If someone else had stopped, people were more likely to, so I pretended to be passing by and would linger and throw some money into the hat—a classic fedora his brother-in-law used to wear to poker games that Kenny's sister said he wouldn't miss. A mom and dad pushing a stroller stopped to hear part of a choppy rendition of Careless Love—first time Kenny played it. This Land is Your Land came next in his repertoire and the new papa tossed in a handful of change. Then, for a while nobody stopped. Kenny had to start over once he had gone through So Long It's Been Good to Know You, The Streets of Laredo, and The Green Green Grass of Home, which sounds pretty sappy until you get to the end and realize the guy's on death row, about to be executed.

When school started there were roving bands of kids in the afternoon. A bunch of them claimed a nearby bench, three sitting across the back with their feet on the seat, all of them talking loud, scaring people away. They started making fun of Kenny and I was about to go over to tell them to buzz off. Kenny grabbed my arm and as I turned to pull away, I locked eyes with this guy coming up the path. He saw what was happening, and he went over to the kids and said something. They were black kids and he was black.

"I said, 'What d'ya all think you're doin?'" he yelled. One of the girls flinched.

"Just having fun," said the boy in the middle.

He told them, "Clear out!" and they did.

He waved me off when I tried to thank him and went on his way. That was the first time we met Marcus.

Thursday night dinner in the basement of St. Paul's, we stood with our plates, looking for a place to sit down and I spotted him at one of the tables. I wasn't sure if he recognized us from the indifferent nod he gave. Nobody was talking; we sat there and ate. He wiped his mouth when he finished and said, "After a good meal I still want a cigarette."

I knew what he meant. "Yeah, I quit three years ago."

"So, how you doin' out there?" he said to Kenny. "Where's your guitar?"

Kenny put down his fork to tell how he'd fallen asleep on the subway, waking up suddenly at his stop and jumped off, not realizing he didn't have the guitar until he was up on the street. Didn't make much money, but it was something he enjoyed. It hurt to lose that guitar. Marcus said, "Sorry." Kenny didn't eat any more of the chicken and rice on his plate and paid no attention when I said that he should. All day we'd only had a muffin and a bowl of soup. "Well, if you're not going to, I think somebody might." I could see Marcus was still hungry.

"Go ahead," said Kenny, sliding his plate over. "I had a big lunch."

A guy sweeping the floor asked us to move, so we went out on The Common, Marcus telling us how he had gone to trade school to be a printer, a job he had twelve years, up until the business folded. "So I figured I'll learn computers, but then most of that gets sent overseas. My brother trained as a medical technician. The pay's all right, but it's not the kind of work I want to be doing. Hospitals give me the creeps."

Kenny told him how he had planned to go to culinary school but the loan didn't come through.

"That's one loan you won't have to pay off," said Marcus.

"Same thing with Chris. She wanted to do physical therapy."

I glanced at Kenny with a flash of annoyance, not wanting to be reminded.

"Good need for that," said Marcus. "Good job security."

"Yeah," I said. I thought the work would be gratifying, something more than a daily grind. I'd be helping people recover, see them get back what they'd had. I didn't want to remember those weeks waiting to hear that I got accepted, and then not get the loan.

We came to the edge of the park. "What are you planning on doing now?" said Kenny.

"Right now? I'm headed to my nephew's, over on Huntington. I'll probably see you around. Chris. Kenny." He walked to the corner, then, turning back and seeing us standing there, he yelled, "You wanna come?"

Kenny and I ran to catch up.

We cut through the Prudential Center, and came down by the fountain at that end of the Christian Science plaza. A hush came over us walking across the open space between the cloister and the long rectangular pool continuously brimming over. Marcus said it was called a reflecting pool because you're supposed to stop and reflect, so we did, standing there listening to the sound of the water.

"Peaceful," I said.

Across the street, Symphony Hall was all lit up. People were spilling out the doors, the men in dark suits, the women in skirts and matching jackets or elegant coats. The performance had just ended and they were coming down the steps, clogging the sidewalk, some of them so wrapped up in conversation they were oblivious to us trying to weave our way through. A woman held both hands to her chest. "That violinist! He took my breath away." A younger man, maybe her son, said, "Brilliant, just brilliant." An old couple crossed our path walking to the curb arm-in-arm, the man handsome and upright, his pure white hair curling over his collar. I didn't care about their fashionable clothes or that they were able to ride off in a cab; I envied how full of life they were.

A few more blocks and we came to the apartment house where

his nephew lived. Nice entrance. Old wood and shiny mailboxes. We followed him up the stairs and down the hall to a big apartment with comfortable chairs and a thick pile rug in the living room. We could take off our shoes, put our feet up and relax. Marcus found a note in the kitchen. His nephew was staying the night at his girl-friend's; we had the place to ourselves. Didn't feel like watching TV, so we put on some music and we just sat there and talked.

Robert came home the next morning, not at all surprised to find two strangers bedded down on his living room rug. After a quick shower and a change of clothes he sat down with us to a breakfast of coffee and toast. Then he was off, he said, to New York for the weekend. We were welcome to stay and finish off the pan of lasagna in the fridge.

Kenny and I had plans to go to the day center and check the job listings. Marcus said he'd come along. My neck was stiff and after two cups of coffee I was still groggy; I'd barely slept. Kenny looked at me across the table and said, "Why don't you stay and rest up."

"Take the bed," said Marcus. "Make yourself at home."

The shades were still drawn, the room dark and cave-like, the unmade bed welcoming. I wondered when the sheets were last changed and laughed that the thought even occurred to me. Ah, the give of the springs underneath as I sat on the edge. I lowered my head to the pillow, stretched out my legs, and slipped off to sleep.

Late in the day I woke up and lay there, under the covers. The bedroom door was open a crack and I could hear the friendly mur-mur of Kenny and Marcus in the kitchen, the intermittent clink of pans and plates. Those comfy sounds of home. If only for a couple days we were warm and safe. And we had food—I could smell the lasagna heating in the oven.

Right from the start, they were like brothers, playfully goading each other like guys do. Marcus picked up on us being equal part-ners, and I appreciated that he didn't put on one face for Kenny and another for me. The two of us made sure he didn't feel like a third wheel, in fact, he sort of balanced us out.

Marcus never made any moves on me and I didn't flirt. The shift happened without discussion, the way things happen in nature. Not the nature you see on Wild Kingdom, where the alpha male edges out the rest; we were at a more basic level. On a weekend back at his nephew's apartment, Kenny and I were in the living room sleeping on a leaky air mattress. I got up without turning on a light and knocked over a glass. Marcus came out to see what broke. The three of us picked up the pieces. Since we were both up, Kenny pumped more air into the mattress. Marcus said for us to switch; we should take the bed.

I remembered what it felt like to sleep in there and tears of exhaustion came to my eyes. Marcus put his arm around me and I leaned against him. Again he offered, "I'll sleep out here."

"No, go ahead," said Kenny.

This wouldn't have happened under normal circumstances. Under normal circumstances you're not in situations like that. Marcus and I went into the room and got into bed. I don't remember it feeling strange. We each stayed on our own side. Before I knew it, I fell asleep and slept the rest of the night.

The next day we went our separate ways: Marcus to his weekend security guard job, Kenny to the lot where he had a gig selling wreaths and Christmas trees. I went to the bookstore that hired seasonal help; it didn't pay much, but everyone was so nice I would have worked there for free.

We had some money, so we went to the supermarket, strolling up and down the aisles, loading the cart with cranberry sauce, pumpkin pie, and stuffing mix; all now on sale. We opted for a roast, having eaten our turkey dinner the week before at St Paul's. Kenny picked out a bottle of wine and we had candles on the table, Bach playing. Kenny made us laugh with stories about the holidays when his uncle Walt used to visit. Still sitting around the table after pie and coffee, Marcus told us about his wife, that she had moved down to Georgia after a miscarriage. "I tried to tell her that can happen for no reason, but the way things were going, that was the last straw."

He leaned forward in his chair, his head bent. Maybe she was better off without him. I don't think he believed that, but there was nothing he could do; he had to let her go. I wondered if he'd gone down and tried to reconcile, but I didn't want to ask, didn't want him to think of leaving. Kenny and I were thankful for Marcus, for his spirit and for the way he made us feel secure. He was thankful for us taking away the loneliness that was starting to get to him after being on his own for three months.

We'd used every pot and pan making our feast. It took an hour cleaning up with me washing and them doing the drying, having to remember which cupboard or drawer to put things away in. They snapped their towels at each other and dueled with a spatula and a serving spoon.

"One of the best Thanksgivings in a long time," said Marcus.

"Even if it was a week late," said Kenny, folding his towel to hang on the rack.

The three of us stood in the middle of the kitchen. A look passed between Kenny and me. Then between Kenny and Marcus. Kenny leaned in to kiss me on the forehead, and said, "Go on, you need your sleep."

That night in the bedroom Marcus and I didn't go straight to sleep. I reached out to him and he took hold of me. Once that happened, there was no back and forth; I could be with one or the other, but not with both. There wasn't much opportunity or inclination, being tired and self-conscious. But that's how things stood the rest of the time the three of us were together, just because life's easier when everyone knows what to expect.

The clatter of a train on the tracks woke us in that big room with the paintings along the wall. We'd slept three across on the futon like spoons; Kenny pressed to my back, and me pressed against Marcus. The coverlet wasn't very warm, so we had piled our coats on top. The clock radio set for six-thirty came on. Kenny bumped against me turning over. I heard the water running in the sink. A kettle whistled. The smell of coffee got me up.

Kenny finishing his mug, setting it on the counter. Mikhail Pavlovich only had two mugs. I poured one for Marcus and one for me. He drank his walking around, looking at the paintings. We folded up the futon and made sure everything was just as we found it.

"Come on." I wanted to get out of there before it got light outside.

"Got the keys?" said Marcus.

"Yep," said Kenny. He locked the door behind us.

Around eight-thirty that night we got off the train and stood on the platform, checking to see if there were any lights in the windows. All clear in back, but in front we could see there was somebody still on the second floor. We waited in a doorway across the street for half an hour before a car pulled up and tooted its horn. The window went dark and a couple minutes later a woman came out.

"Maybe she knows where Mikhail Pavlovich is," I said, watching the taillights turn the corner.

"Sure, somebody knows," said Kenny.

The keys we had made worked fine. We took another look at the alarm, just to reassure ourselves, whispering as we went up the steps. On the landing with the giant caterpillar we stopped to hear complete silence. I hadn't been nervous the night before walking down the hall, but now I was. We came to the door and Kenny un-locked it.

"Honey, I'm home."

"Shh."

Marcus closed the door, laughing at Kenny, or at me for being so jumpy.

We pulled the space heater over so we could sit down and get warm. I said, "Maybe if we talked to someone we could find out where Mikhail is or when he's expected back."

We came up with a plan for me to be standing in the entrance tomorrow, ringing Mikhail's bell. Somebody was bound to come in, maybe see which bell I was ringing, and they might just tell me what we wanted to know.

The bakery around the corner opened early. We sat at the window watching people passing by. What time did artists go to work? Kenny figured they'd roll in around ten. He finished his coffee and headed off to the Manpower office. Marcus went to his weekend security job and went to check in with personnel about getting more hours. The three of us would meet at the Dunkin Donuts on Washington Street, and if we had the money, we'd go to Chinatown instead of the weekly church dinner.

Inside the building's entrance I took up my post by the door-bells. Wouldn't it be weird if I rang the bell and somebody answered. I didn't have a watch, but it seemed like a long time before a burly guy in a motorcycle jacket yanked the outer door open and passed by. I waited some more and there were two girls talking to each other, carrying stuff in. Again I heard the door open behind me and I stretched out my hand, pressing the bell for number twelve.

"Oh, are you looking for Mik?" said a woman's voice. "He's still in the hospital." She had long white hair and a face that was old and pretty.

"He is, still?"

"I think the operation went all right. But then he got some infection, so they had to keep him." She rummaged in her purse as she spoke. "I'm not sure when he's getting out."

"What an ordeal. I was just stopping by, I didn't realize."

She pulled out her keys. "He's still in Mass General."

"Oh, thanks."

"Doesn't sound like he's getting out in the next couple days," said Marcus. "And when he does, he'll still be recovering."

We were finishing up our bowls of noodle soup. Kenny pushed back from the table and said, "All we have to do is check in with Mass General every morning to see if he's been released."

We stopped to pick up some pastries for breakfast. We were standing in line—everybody around us speaking Chinese—and I barely heard Marcus say, "Me and Lorraine used to stop in here after dinner." On the way home he was quiet. He got moody like that sometimes; Kenny and I would just let him be.

This time, going into the building I was relaxed. If we ran into anybody, hell, we were Mik's friends. We checked the mailbox— keeping it empty so nobody would have to bring up the contents. I put some water on the hot plate to boil. Mik had a selection of teas and we could all have some at the same time since I'd stopped at the Goodwill down the street and picked up another mug.

"I wish I had that guitar," said Kenny. He switched on the radio and we heard the forecast for tomorrow: freezing rain turning to snow.

Marcus pulled on the cardigan in the style of a smoking jacket that he'd found at the free store. He tied the sash, walking along the paintings propped against the wall, over to the table where there was a hubcap holding smears of dried paint and brushes laid out in a row. One by one, he picked up the brushes, getting a feel for each, running it along the table top. Kenny and I sat on the couch, leafing through the art magazines. "Get a load of this." Marcus twisted the gooseneck lamp to shine on the row of paintings—all dark and abstract—moving them around so he could see them. Several were indistinguishable from a distance, but if you went up close, you could

see the little dots and squiggles. He found a blank canvas—maybe
that's what he was looking for—and set it on the easel.

Kenny turned in early, making his own bed over by the kitchen
with flat pieces of foam he'd found in a packing crate on the back
stairs. I unfolded the couch and Marcus came over later, after Kenny
was snoring.

The next morning we had milk for coffee and ate the almond
cookies. Marcus stared out the window at the wet snow coming
down. Then he was standing in front of the blank canvas. Kenny and
I watched him squeeze out daubs of paint onto a piece of cardboard.
He picked up a brush.

"What happened to leaving everything just as we found it?"
Kenny muttered.

Marcus kept adding to the array of colors he applied, covering
the canvas. He got so absorbed in what he was doing I don't think he
heard Kenny say, "You missed a spot."

Kenny shrugged and put on his jacket; he had to get to work. At
the door he glanced back at me.

"I think I'll wait 'til it lets up," I said. There was no place I had
to be that early, so I indulged in the luxury of sitting by the space
heater, curled up with a gardening book I'd found. My mind was like
a dog with a bone, always gnawing on ways we might have kept the
apartment. Or dreaming of the place we would have as soon as we
could scrape together the rent. I got lost in the gardening book's big
glossy photographs; the colors so vivid I imagined myself walking
among rows of columbine and larkspur.

At the day center I spent a couple hours sifting through the job listings. Three of the places had already hired. Another one I called said
to come in tomorrow. On the way home I thought of Kenny all day
on that construction site. The sun had come out and melted some of
the snow that had fallen, but still it was cold.

Coming home—that's how it felt walking from the train. Like
anyone else with a key to the place, I smiled and said hello to the
guy I passed in the hall. Maybe they all knew about us, and it was all
right with them; we weren't causing any trouble.

I came in the door and Marcus was standing by the window, still
painting, the last of the sun streaming into the room around him.
He scooped me up in his arms and we twirled around, falling dizzy

and laughing onto the couch. He just felt good and wanted to share it. After all the things we'd lost or couldn't have, what a relief to know we could still feel like that.

A key turned in the lock and I tensed at the sound of the door opening.

"Hey Kenny," Marcus called out. Of course it was Kenny.

My father used to come home, drained and irritable from work, demanding quiet from his noisy children who had no understanding of his daily sacrifice. Kenny came around to stand in front of us, his face weather-beaten from working outside. He held up the bag of takeout from the Mexican down the street. He was just glad to be home.

"Hey, what's going on?" he said. He sat down on the couch to take off his boots and sighed.

"Tough day?"

"Yeah."

"I'll make some tea," I said. "I just got home myself."

"Hey, not bad," said Kenny, having a look at the canvas.

There were smudges and jots of every color, abstract but not off-putting like the other paintings. It had brightness and energy. I didn't understand it any more than I understood the ones by Mikhail Pavlovich. From the way Marcus looked at it, he didn't either, his mouth slightly open, his eyes roaming the mysterious landscape he had made.

"I think you've got something here," said Kenny.

"Yeah, you might consider taking it up," I said.

"I think that'll be it," said Marcus. He opened the bag Kenny had set on the counter.

We took our Goodwill plates and sat on the couch facing the windows, watching the last of the daylight pull away. Kenny brought a quart of beer—a little splurge—and we filled our mugs. This was all anyone could want, a full stomach and the space heater glowing like a fire in a hearth. At first Kenny just grunted when asked about work; once he'd downed his burrito, he told us about the motley crew at the job site. "I learned how to say hammer and nails in Portuguese. How 'bout you? Any luck at the day center?"

"There's a place I'm gonna check out tomorrow." I got up to take our plates to the sink.

"You remember to call the hospital?"

"Yep, he's still there."

The next morning Marcus went off to the Spare Change office for some papers to sell. Kenny went back to the construction job. I went to see the manager at Bill's Grill. He had already hired a waitress but there was an opening in the kitchen. Minimum wage. He said I could start tomorrow. I wanted so bad to be able to say I found a job.

No tips in the kitchen, but at least I could eat. Off at 3:00, I went to the library until it was time to meet up at the church for dinner. During my break I called the hospital and the lady said she didn't have any Mikhail Pavlovich on the patient list. I asked if he'd been released and she said, "That's all the information I have."

"That could mean one of two things," said Kenny. "Let's assume he just got out. He won't be getting back to work right away."

On Saturday Marcus went to his security job. Kenny was going to his sister's to borrow her electric grill so he could cook a dinner. He needed me to go along to carry stuff. We spent some time with Nora and the kids, then picked up a few things at the store. We were back before it got dark.

One of the girls I had seen that day I stood ringing the doorbell was going out as we came in with our groceries and the grill. She barely noticed us. It was all quiet in the hallway. Kenny unlocked the door, stepped inside, and stopped short.

I came around him to see a frail old man in a wheelchair sitting in the middle of the room. His body rotated with his head as if fused.

"Come in," he said, in a mechanical voice, the words coming through a devise in his throat. A woman sat off to the side with a magazine in her lap.

"My nurse," he said.

A tight covering of pale white skin covered the bones in his face. He had no hair and his eyes grew large as he sputtered trying to speak. He leaned his head back, motoring over to the nurse with her box of gauze pads. She replaced the one taped to his throat with another; it took a second. He rolled a few inches then stopped, his eyes fixed on the mug he didn't recognize on the counter, then over to where the two of us stood at attention.

"So, you've been looking after the place," he said, the irony magnified by the metallic flatness of the half-human voice.

Kenny chuckled. "Yeah, we've been looking after things."

He peered at me. "How'd you get in?"

"There was an open window."

"Open window," he echoed. Then, "I'll take the keys."

Kenny dropped his into the outstretched hand, looking over at me, probably wondering, like I was, if he'd ask for mine. That look didn't escape the old man. I might have told him I didn't have any keys, but with those death ray eyes staring out of that skull-at me, he snapped his fingers and I handed them over. His wheel bumped the groceries I'd set down and he stared at the feathery green top of the fennel sticking out of the bag.

Back to the middle of the room, he pulled up near the space heater. "Nobody bothered you?"

"No, sir."

"Warm enough?"

"Better than being outside," I said.

He rolled up and down in front of the paintings, lingering to look at the one that wasn't his. Kenny went over to him and the chair shot backwards. I think he accidently pushed the button. Repositioned, he turned his body toward Kenny. "Yours?" he said.

"Marcus did that."

He said something that came out garbled. The nurse went to him, but he lifted his hand, to show he didn't need her. Like somebody pacing, he went to and fro, then stopped and turned abruptly. We heard the jangle of keys he tossed on the counter. "You can stay," he said.

I got up the nerve to ask, "When will you be coming back to work?"

Without another word he motioned to the nurse, and she went to open the door, very businesslike, not giving any hint of what she thought about us. He buzzed out into the hall.

At first Marcus didn't believe it when Kenny told him. Once I convinced him we weren't making it up, he didn't react the way we thought he would.

"He said we could stay," Kenny repeated, turning to me, exasperated.

"Maybe we can sleep here at night and he could come and paint during the day," I said, but still no reaction.

"Your painting caught his attention," said Kenny, trying to get a rise out of him. "'Ve-ry in-ter-est-ing'—that's what he said."

"Yeah?" said Marcus, slightly amused.

"You'll be able to ask him yourself when he comes back around."

Only, Mikhail Pavlovich wouldn't be coming back; that was the other thing Kenny and I hadn't understood. He'd been released from the hospital with a hospice nurse and was visiting his studio for the last time. Two weeks later we would come up the stairs with our groceries and be stuck in the hall, trying our keys that no longer worked because the lock had been changed.

That night Kenny served up pork chops grilled with strips of red peppers, fresh fennel, and onions with rice. We took our plates over to the couch, Marcus sitting quietly between us. Our staying there was supposed to be temporary and the idea that it didn't have to be as temporary as we thought—the very thing that made Kenny and me so happy—didn't matter to him.

He sat upright, preoccupied; while Kenny and I lounged, basking in the permission that had been granted. We had landed on a cushioned ledge that kept us from falling, and for now, this was ours. Marcus had other ideas. Something had come unstuck in him, and he had to go, move, get back up to where he could see above ground to what lay ahead.I woke up during the night and he wasn't there. He'd put on his coat, taken the gooseneck lamp over to the desk and was bent over the circle of light, writing a letter. He had made up his mind to go see Lorraine and plead with her to take him back. He sent the letter and didn't wait for a reply. It was so sudden, him leaving like that.

Kenny and I now have our own place, a tiny one bedroom in the basement of an old brick building in Dorchester. We're glad for our own space and the heat—there's lots of it—and a real kitchen with an oven and a stove. Our own bathroom where we can take a shower anytime. We joked how it would seem strange at first, just the two of us, but I'm waitressing and Kenny has two jobs, so we're almost never both here.

In the subway last night, I thought I saw Marcus on the other platform. He was the same height and moved like Marcus. The train on that track came in and I walked down to look through the windows into the cars at the people getting on. It pulled out before I had a chance to see his face. Another time at the restaurant I thought I saw him walk by the window, and I wanted to run to the door and call out his name.

But it couldn't have been Marcus. He's down in Atlanta with Lorraine.

Kaitlin Jennrich

Mirror

Of course, after her stepmother had gone dancing into a burning grave, the queen still had to destroy every trace of her from the palace. Out went her ridiculous gowns, all tulle and satin and absurdly stitched flowers. Out went the lotions and ointments, the small vials of perfume and darkly burbling liquid. Out went the four-poster bed, the golden cups, the rugs. Her fiancé coordinated the piles of flaming furniture and tried not to ask too many questions; he blamed the queen's newfound obsession with spring cleaning on the early loss of a father figure, the poisonous relationship with her stepmother, those defining years spent raised by dwarves. The servants pointed out that her stepmother had, after all, tried to kill her three or four times. The townspeople told him that the queen hadn't had very many happy memories in that castle, the poor thing. Her fiancé nodded along while secretly mourning the loss of a very fine set of hunting knives, wickedly sharpened to perfection. The queen didn't care. She watched it all burn from the highest tower. If she had a god, she thought, it would be the swirls of smoke rising past the pale blue sky and beyond.

She saved the mirror for last.

The mirror tried, of course, to convince her otherwise. It told her she was beautiful, a fact of which she was already well aware. It showed her lands beyond the reaches of the kingdom, past the diamond mountains and the black canyons, and claimed it could help her conquer them; she had no use for additional countries that would only require more bureaucracy. It warned her that her fiancé was flighty, unreliable, and far too innocent, and that she would require the mirror to keep him in check. She laughed and said her fiancé was the least of her worries.

Finally, the mirror showed her one last image—its best hand. A raven-haired girl sat on the forest floor. Light fell like gold dust through the trees and settled on her shoulders. Her skin was as white as the snow. The huntsman fell to his knees before her. She had kissed him, once, a long time ago; the raven-haired girl in the mirror and the queen both raised their hands to their lips, and considered.

"And what?" said the queen to the mirror. "What can this possibly mean?"

"Every good ruler needs a heart," said the mirror in an old, cracked voice. "I can be yours."

The queen reached out a finger to touch the surface of the mirror. She could see her reflection in the scene playing out on the mirror—the girl reached out a hand to touch the huntsman while her head tilted up towards the sky, and the sun. Her face was older now, more savage, but just as lovely. The queen carefully took the mirror off of the wall, and then, after a moment of adjusting, threw it against the floor. Glass shattered. With the heel of her boot, she ground every shard into the stone until nothing was left but a fine, silvery powder. Then she gathered all the powder up in her hands and blew it out the window until it joined with the wreathing smoke columns in the sky.

After all, it would never do to see what happened next. That kind of information in the hands of her fiancé, or her advisors, or her vassals—inconceivable. But now who was left to know what she had done? How she had taken the huntsman's knife and measured the weight of it, carefully considering, before finally pressing it against her skin? How she had cut a small slit just under her breastbone, felt the cool kiss of steel sliding past her lungs? How her chest had snapped and burned when she plucked her own heart from behind her rib cage and brought it beating into the light? How curious she had felt afterwards, light and strange and pure, but just as empty as before—how the huntsman could hardly stand to look at her, yet couldn't drag his eyes away? She had handed her heart to him, still thumping unevenly, and smiled in her best approximation of kindness.

"Here," she had said. "You can take this to the queen."

No, it was best that the memory remain a secret. And since her stepmother had taken care of the huntsman once his presumed treachery was discovered, the queen could finally rule in peace. Just once, looking out the window of the highest tower, did she allow herself to think about that day for the last time in many, many years: warm sunlight in her hair, the dark blue of the huntsman's eyes, the scent of iron and blood on the wind, and her heartbeat, like a war drum, pounding long after it had left her hands.

But that was a long time ago, and so much had happened since then. The queen dusted the last remains of the mirror off of her skirt, closed the tower window, and went down to join her fiancé in watching the rest of her stepmother burn.

Carrie Meadows

Telling

The wheat has survived the winter frost. For two months it has grown taller and greener by the day and, for two months, Grampa has been bringing Kaley here. Every Sunday he plans to tell her. He drags her along, understanding that she would rather do anything in this world on a Sunday afternoon than walk through the wheat field.

"Wheat," he says. "Is the purest form of food." He looks out over the field, thinking how just last fall he held the seeds in his hands. Now the stalks are as tall as Kaley's shoulders.

Kaley looks up, lifting her arm to shield her eyes from the sun. "Why not corn or green beans?"

"Because it's wheat." Grampa's voice is shaky against the back of his throat.

This morning while Kaley walked down the dirt drive for the Sunday paper, her mamma fell getting out of bed. Hearing the thud, Grampa sprung from his rocker, and he scooped his daughter into his arms. He held her steady with his left hand, his fingers sinking deep into the space above her hipbone. With his right arm, he cradled the tendons on the undersides of her knees.

"I'm all right," she said. "You can put me down." She pressed her nose against his chest. Grampa whispered, "I love you, girl. I don't know what I'll do."

She tightened her eyebrows together and said, "Don't go depressing me, Daddy." He carried her to the couch.

Her mamma sat up straight when Kaley came in, but she slouched against the back of the couch as Kaley read *Garfield* and *Blondie* out loud. Grampa leaned forward on his toes and watched the points of his daughter's shoulders shake under her robe as she laughed. She stood up to get Kaley a glass of water but sat quickly, her knees buckling.

Kaley scooted to the opposite side of the couch. She crossed her arms and closed her eyes. Knowing he couldn't put it off any longer, Grampa towed Kaley by one arm through the front door to the wheat field.

The wheat stands strong in the spring breeze. Grampa waves his hand across the tops of the plants, letting their silky heads tickle his fingers.

"Stick your face into it Kaley, the wheat," he says. He puts his hand on her back. "Just take a peek."

"There's bees." Kaley squeezes the bump on her nose where a bee stung her the day before. She frames the spot with her thumb and the knuckle of her index finger until her whole nose is red.

"That's part of it," Grampa says.

Kaley releases her nose and stomps one foot down in front of her grandfather. "Race you home."

Grampa's long arms reach for the girl. He draws her into him before she can make for the house. "Got to tell you something," he says. Grampa tightens his hold and pulls Kaley against the bib of his overalls. She twists her hips to loosen his grip.

"Kaley, listen to me." Grampa cups her shoulders and spins her around. He follows her eyes as they shift from the neighbor's cow pasture to the pond where a few ducks squawk. Kaley narrows her eyelids with stubbornness she learned from her mamma.

Grampa's eyes water at the corners, but he holds tight to Kaley. He kneels on one knee and presses his palms to her cheeks. "Your mamma—" Grampa rubs his tongue along the back of his front teeth. He looks over her head and into the sun until the tops of the wheat appear blurred and spotty. He hooks his thumbs around the straps of his overalls and says, "She's dying."

Grampa reaches out for her, but Kaley is already running for the house, her hands tightened into fists and her pigtails swishing back and forth.

It'll take her a good ten minutes to reach the house, and Grampa knows his words will burn in Kaley's ears as she runs. He knows too that once home, she'll crawl into bed with her mamma and make her promise nothing's wrong. Her mamma will whisper, "Hush child, hush," but the words won't brighten the dull white of her cheek, nor will they erase the picture he knows Kaley has already started to hold in her head: her mamma's skin melting off her bones like the last spoonfuls of honey dripping from a wax comb.

Once Kaley has cried herself to sleep, her mamma will come out of her bed with all the rage of dying in her. She'll unload a bushel of fury on her daddy and wave her arms until she can't catch her breath. She'll tell him to mind his business, not hers. She'll sleep for days at a time, her body growing weaker.

Kaley will begin to follow Grampa into the field, and by late June, she'll run ahead and shout how the wheat has turned from green to gold. They'll prepare the combine for harvest and look for the heads of the wheat to weaken and nod. Grampa and Kaley will come together to watch over the wheat and to worry over Kaley's mamma. They'll make such a fuss, she'll leave the house for walks she's not up to, her back bent from the weight of her head like the dried wheat stalks around her. One day she'll lie against a mossy patch of earth at the edge of the field and pass in her sleep.

Kaley grows small in the distance, and Grampa has to squint to see her sling her sneakers onto the porch step. The sun works at his neck, stiffening the skin and drawing sweat. He knows how the story will go once Kaley's inside the house, and he carries the knowledge deep as the cracks in his knuckles, heavy as the mud caked in his boots. More, he understands that this is practice for Kaley, practice for working in her own calluses. He places his hands on his chest to feel the pump of blood, the click and sputter of life in him despite all he has lost, all he will lose. Most of the time he thinks memory's enough to keep a man's head up. Most of the time, he believes happiness, no matter how far it moves into the past, can keep Kaley safe too. But today—today he feels the wheat closing around him.

Charles O'Hay

The Disposable Life of Keenan Broome

His father was a longshoreman's whistle, his mother a bout of low
self-esteem. He was born in a bucket of rusty nails but, being one
who thrived on neglect, stumbled into manhood on a diet of sucker
punches and raw eggs. "All I ever wanted," he once told the Gunner's
Mate, "was to be a light on Broadway." And after three tours on the
Jack of Clubs and a stint as a sigh of railroad steam, he got a job as
a bulb in the marquee at the Orpheum. Every Saturday night, while
the dancing girls kicked the stars from the sky, you could see him up
there, burning.

Charles O'Hay

Discord in the Hinterland

Each day the news from the provinces was worse. The dolphins were dying. The bees were dying. There were shortages of ice and wheat. The magistrate knew his wife was keeping secrets. Some even from herself. With the passing weeks they spoke less and less. There was pressure to meet the state quotas. In the capital, the trees were whispering secession. Two mockingbirds had been shot while attempting to escape across the river. A mystic was summoned from the hills but was assailed by bandits en route. The magistrate questioned his wife about the note he discovered beneath her pillow. The next day she ran off with a dolphin. He, with a bee.

Chad Prevost

Romantic Poet Cures Himself with Existentialism

I couldn't take myself anywhere
without falling in love.
One day it was the cappuccino girl
who made a flower in the foam,
and then I lost myself for hours
near the bikini girl
playing doubles volleyball,
and only a little later
it was the bookstore clerk
who helped me find
the Early Romantics.
She and her goofy smile
and bottle-eyed glasses.
Then there were the sisters
by the Picasso museum,
and the older woman who gave me
directions through her smoke
and broken English.
I wanted to stop falling in love
all the time so I did the laundry
and hung it on the line
and watched it dry
in Barcelona's seaside air.
I thought of all the lost souls
floating through the wet clothes
empty and alone
and never knowing if
they'd missed anything at all.
The next day I went back out
and found Bookstore Girl
and asked her to marry me.
She said she'd prefer
to start with a poem
and a camping trip

outside the Trappist Monastery.
I didn't ask why or what poem.
We dined on grapes
and watermelon and she read,
"I Wandered Lonely as a Cloud,"
which is about the worst
romantic poem I'd ever heard,
but I bit my lip
and let her go on saying
her flowery things, wishing
I'd proposed to Cappuccino Girl instead.
That night, I slipped away,
changed my name,
and moved to Lisbon
where I wrote heteronyms every day
and only fell in love with
the loneliness of my many selves
flitting in the air like laundry
and clouds, and I grew old
and never wondered again
if I had missed out on anything.

Chad Prevost

Visitation

I began at his favorite haunt,
the café on the Rua dos Douredouras.
I ate alone in the corner like a shadow in the shadows
in search of a shadow
beneath the fado singer's song drifting through
the window. I lost myself.
I forgot who I was.
It was as if I became an empty shell
with room to feel Portugal's invisible
sadness. I was no one and nothing
but the feeling of sadness that reaches out
like a cat's tongue
from the highest *miradoura*
and scours you clean.
That is what I thought as I ate my sandwich
and drank my bottle of wine.
I have been alone many days now
trying to find the man who was no one,
and perhaps the fleeting moment
with the owner asking me if I were okay, perhaps
there in that moment in time in fact
his soul did sweep through me, but that is not
what I sought. I nodded to the man
and moved on down the street, staring up
into the fourth floor windows searching for his face.

Chad Prevost

Things as They Are

To liberate the mind from belief
you must believe in the extinction
of liberation. The beehive's
honeycombed queen
and factory workers. And if you believe
to not believe, to see things
only as they are
without comparison
you must let go of healing
even in the face of certain death.
You will let go of a single god.
You will let go of belief in the world
animated by nothing but gods.
Stones float without air.
Only breath depends on air.
And you will find
just as you were nothing
before you became a soul,
so you will be now as a soul
and there will be no more need
to be anything
and whether or not it makes life
more beautiful
to believe so
doesn't matter.
Things are as they are.
The shadow crossing through
to the next floor.
The cat sleeping in its light.

Sally Roundhouse

Incantation for the Drought

Jehovah, listen, fuck your heels. Wash your needless
soda down as Anton, marionette, tampon,
opal, Anton, marionette, cud, dwellows. Very
ocean liner. Wallop soccer-ball-tomb-miasma.
Yer cankle teats are v. chimera grimalkin
leaflets. In order to nurture my acre mitt,
hens all wasted koatamundi and tapas off. Waft
le either wurst minecraft or homie Sulia.
Oh pin oak angel-beast. Sutton Hoo jackdaw-thrills
a trigger, will owe among onions. How are old
skies pocketing awning's amber? To be awful.

Sally Roundhouse

Incantation for the Junk

Hey Mom, it's that rough frolic, crop-top, knock-knock,
corpuscular shrub rushed the sleep-in, skyrocket,
pig-cupid's wisdom wing-ed total sea. How low
the moist bro eggshell. Gestation month of May. Be
alien, stupid. Arrested animal moan
stuffs velocity's gas mask. Aye, aye! Trundle nearer
tasty profane for nest face. Later, shield naked
Luddite tennis. Then Wicca-call canker sores, entree pimento in
lotus. Arpeggio scuzzins hover over
thirty twats, bid soft brain, bloodstained, tattered pout, laid
out strata with all those rustling, wrinkling, swallows.
I crinkle sphinx visor. Pill pop the church bells, wet almost
green gel, L.A. Look, widowhood's atom groaning.

Sally Roundhouse

Incantation for the Men

Ho Gotham pewing haws. Adan's bone lonely but
Danzig's a cashew. Horizon thunders Matthew.
Dank skanks skank. Men who pause Finnegan warble blessed
this bath. Oh so mysterio, so you waves
wind my wind. Kamikaze on the under cover.
Juke joint sweater near ox blood, blue texture. Water
parts of obliterated. Ahh men. Kiss, kiss wharves
weave Lamar's kitchen garden, Demopolis, blue
geese through neap tide, hell oxygen. Nope socks grin. Call
me mosquito muscle. Dope soap, Soap.

Sally Roundhouse

Incantation for the Widower

These is envelopes, pilose, dicegloat, swallow gown
desert rat. Arrow a single deserter warbles
ire. You ermine sashimi yellow empire
woast: drove loaves to drizzle of bread lanterns, break every
crucible worth deferring. Burrow as other ghosts
truffle. Unlucky oar sees urchin that the nom
de furrow guzzles, and ladies roam of town thin
tubal. Oh corrosive wunderskate. Is that old
Neanderthal, then, under water? So facto
tum-tum strum equestrian wrung. Icarus is
dunderhead.

Robert Joe Stout

An Invitation He Couldn't Refuse

To hear Matt Morrison talk you might believe that he'd created the poet/publisher/Gatherer-of-the-Tribes that he claimed to be out of sheer will and fortitude but in fact his life was a pool ball knocked here and there by forces he seldom perceived nor understood. Stubby forefinger darting here and there as though dotting dozens of invisible i's he would pontificate "the great shamans believed…" before sliding into clichés about the Earth Mother and her children, bemoan society's disregard of "real" poetry and hit you up for a contribution. Or a meal. Or a place to sleep.

Not that Matt was inert flotsam without gumption or volition. He was in fact a bit pushy in his hat-pulled-over-his-eyes backwoodsy way. For the nearly thirty years that he'd been a poet/publisher/Gatherer-of-the-Tribes he'd harangued, begged, cajoled, imposed broadsides, pamphlets, CDs and open mic appearances on hundreds of students, poetasters, publishers and coffeehousers in towns and cities from North Carolina to his "spiritual homeland" Berkeley (although he didn't live in Berkeley but fifteen or twenty busstops away in a predominately Mexican barrio in Oakland).

Had you been in the student hangout near a university campus in northern California one shivery evening in early December he might have hit you up because—as happened all too frequently—he was stranded. In his all-so-friendly hey-we're-all-brothers way he would have explained that the woman he'd thought could be a soul mate had led him to believe that the university would pay him to participate in a poetry presentation. The university—that is to say a little campus non-profit organization affiliated with the university—did pay him but not very much and the prospective soul mate told him to get lost because she misunderstood his suggesting that she take him home with her for the night.

"I wasn't hitting on her. I hadn't lined up a place to stay and thought, you know, a couch, something like that," he explained to three graduate student types who looked like they might be interested in poets/publishers/Gatherers-of-the-Tribe.

They weren't but suggested that "Elizabeth" knew a lot of hippie-artist-theater types who sometimes went to poetry readings. Elizabeth turned out to be the manager/cashier/waitress, a wispy blonde with wing-tipped glasses and faintly freckled cheeks.

With that semi-sophisticated air of a longtime student/dropout/reapply Elizabeth conceded that the coffeehouse sometimes hosted music or "artsy" events.

"Won-der-ful!" Matt responded in his sweetest Car'lina lisp and from a backpack crammed with copies of the last three issues of his poetry rag, CDs featuring Tribes readings and a bagfull of dirty socks extracted half-a-dozen rumpled but readable fliers featuring Matt Morrison readings, chantings and declamations.

Elizabeth, duly under-impressed, took them and shrugged. "Nhh, maybe we can work something out. How long are you going to be in town."

Matt shuffled a quirky two-step and explained that he wasn't sure, he hadn't lined up a place to say.

"Twelfth Street house," one of the grad student types interrupted. The two with him laughed but Elizabeth shrugged.

"Why not? You seem to be their type."

"What's the Twelfth Street house?"

"Twelve blocks straight west, half a block to your left. Big brass ship's bell hanging over the front door."

Why a big brass ship's bell would be hanging over the door seemed a bit disconcerting but Matt wasn't one to ruminate about such things. Before he left the coffeehouse he thumbtacked one of his fliers to its bulletin board and promised Elizabeth he'd be back for more "great French roast." She jammed a half bagel in the toaster behind the counter without answering. Knowing what student/dropout/reapplies were like Matt didn't take it as a brush off or lack of interest. Pack over his back he headed west.

The town's hip boutique and chia and wine hangouts gave way to bead shop and bike repair fringe businesses before he got to the Twelfth Street corner: an old Dairy Queen converted into a liquor store with a steamy taco wagon parked in front. Matt hesitated, then just past a green-awninged warehouse detected what looked like a two-story beached Mississippi River paddlewheeler with a big brass bell hanging over the front porch. Adjusting his hat and Car'lina smile "Here we go" he murmured and headed towards the sagging front porch. As he shifted his backpack from one shoulder to the other one of the four front steps gave way beneath him and he lurched forward, the pack cracking the back of his head and knocking his hat over his eyes.

"Damn step. We've been meaning to fix the fucker. You okay?"

Hands against the top step Matt pushed himself half upright. A barefooted twenty-something swung out of the hammock tied to the front post pillar to peer at him.

"Startled me. I wasn't lookin', I guess."

"Nhh, no problem."

A bit taken aback that the twenty-something didn't ask who he was or what he wanted Matt introduced himself "poet...reading at the university...Elizabeth in the coffeehouse..."

"Sure, fine, go on in."

Matt hesitated, then offered a "thanks buddy" and pulled open the creaky screen door. "Hi," he heard but none of those shuffling through the makeshift livingroom made a point of approaching him. Feeling he needed to establish his identity Matt explained his Gatherer-of-the-Tribes poetness singularly and plurally to a widehipped teenager who appeared to be the twenty-something's girlfriend, a stumpy bespectacled hulk mumbling about student teaching, a wiry hyperactive type who claimed to be an actor and half-a-dozen others who lived in the paddlewheeler, hung out there or were friends of those who did.

"Lizbeth is okay," a just-returned-from-Afghanistan re-entree affirmed, "a bit tight-assed but okay." The others agreed, merging in and out of half-a-dozen conversations that seemed to involve everyone but no one in particular but that confirmed that Matt was welcome to crash and could have "the rug."

"The rug" turned out to be a braided afghan sewn or pegged to a dilapidated mattress tossed on the floor of a somewhat screened in back porch. Not the Hyatt but comfortable enough for one who'd slept on harder surfaces more than once in his life. Matt thanked what seemed to be the leaderless gathering and chipped in for burritos and a big bag of corn chips that the self-proclaimed actor brought from the taco stand. Other than one scrawny mophead who conceded that peddling poetry might be "an okay gig" none of the dozen or more paddlewheeler in-and-outers conceded more than a minute or two to Matt's tribal gatherings but bags of peanuts appeared along with half-pail of knobby green apples, the twenty-something twittered with a guitar and the student teacher hulk brought out a bong. Content, if a big confused by clattering surrounding him, Matt laughed, took a few hits, shared stories and as the interchanges diminished in tone and intensity made his way to the rug to chant himself contentedly to sleep.

The ship's bell's clanging shattered his dreaming.

"Raid! Raid! Raid!"

Matt shoved his feet into his shoes, grabbed his pack and blundered out the back door. The clanging had stopped but an alarm, apparently in the liquor store, was screeching. Half-crouching, half-running he scurried towards the warehouse but stepped on his own shoestring and plunged across a thistly patch of dying grass. As he pushed himself to his feet a brilliant white light enveloped him.

"Stay right where you are."

Two forms approached him, one on either side.

"Let's see your I.D.," the one on his left gruffed, voice more bored than threatening.

"I, well, you see..." Matt forced himself to take a deep breath, trying to find within his temporary panic a bit of Car'lina charm, "I have here my, ah, food stamp certifica—"

"Driver's license," the voice on his right, hoarse but feminine, interrupted.

"A while back, see, my car broke down and without it I couldn't renew..." Aware his explanation was getting him nowhere Matt spread his hands to show the two cops his harmlessness and good will and explained that he was just visiting, he was a poet and—

"Oh Jesus, another one of those," the female voice muttered. The male voice laughed. Matt started to explain how well his poetry had been received but the twenty-something's voice interrupted.

"He's stayin' with us."

"You get 'em all, don't you?"

The twenty-something laughed. As he looked around for the others Matt realized that he was the only one of the Paddle-wheelers who'd fled the building.

"Damn kids, it's the third time this month—"

"Yeah, they also set off the liquor store alarm." The female cop checked a call on her radio and slid it back onto her belt. Matt looked down at his still untied shoes

"I was so sound asleep when I heard the clanging I—"

Neither of the cops was listening. Hat pushed back from his high forehead the male cop walked a few steps towards the paddlewheeler beside the twenty-something and the female cop turned towards Matt.

"Not the best place in the world to stay. You'd do better at Salvation Army."

Matt cleared his throat and grinned. "Made an invitation I couldn't rightly refuse," he exaggerated his Car'lina drawl. The female cop groaned and the male cop laughed and Matt swung his pack off his shoulder. Before either of them could turn away:

"Y'know, I've got some great CDs here. Native chants, Gathers-of-the-Tribes. Maybe you'd like to buy—?"

Abigail Uhrick

Brood Parasites

I.

It is your job to stalk the chaparral, breath catching
as you glimpse the corner of one wire cage—holding in
air until habitation or absence is obvious.
The Tijuana River rumbles less quickly
than your blood when the muted earthen head
twitches within the metal confines—muddy wings
lashing to purchase lift. This bird will not be able to lay
her eggs in another's nest.

Mother left you with the neighbor, who every day forced you
to stay in a straight-backed chair in front of the picture
window like the stiff doll you once saw sitting on a man's
lap talking to a crowd. That was when your aunt took you along
to Santa Monica—the electric pier at dark, the dense and
shouting streets. Back home, mother sent you to the neighbor's
again with five dollars for his time. He told you that you might
as well call him Daddy.

II.

You slide the cage, with thickly gloved hands, into the bright
tent-like bag, attaching the tube to a hole in the covering and to your
own exhaust. The bird is not calm under the dark covering, as if she
senses that this is not the time for sleep. She does not know
her mistakes, her sins. You start the car and look at your watch—
fifteen minutes. The high frequency squeak like reticent ice cracking
and the frenzied slap of feathers against plastic stop after seven. As you do
for every dead thing, you make the sign of the cross.

Mother is immobile in an institutional bed—tubes bringing in
air and nutrients and eliminating what is left behind, sustaining
life. The marks of age glint like stubborn spots of rust on the translucent

tissue of her cheeks. She chatters under her breath, to only herself, the soft *keks* warbled in resignation at having to stay. You sit next to her lowered bed, your gloves in the pocket of your coat, your car keys jingling nervously between two fingers. You think of your old neighbor. You look at your watch.

Abigail Uhrick

We Are Biodynamic

Dandelion, horsetail, and the skull of a domesticated animal—he says he has found
the combination and promises with words like fecund and lush. But it is
she who remembers to bring the cow's horn, and the smooth, cold facets
of the quartz slide on the chain around her neck against only slightly warmer skin. It is
she who crushes the crystal to dust, fills the horn, and digs. It is she who digs again
and sprays to prevent the wrong things from growing.

He whispers efficacy into her ear as she sleeps; he breathes yield
through open windows. Yet it is she who charts the moon and watches the patterns
the stars create. She solely knows what must be harvested and when—in the coil
of the crab, vulnerability; in the impact of a ram, control. She is the one who ensures
the seeds continue to germinate while he only spills evaporating exclamations
and big-picture plans.

She knows words can cause sprouting and flowering. She is certain
of increase—of infusion from magic to fruit. She composts the necessary elements
of he, of she, and the mixture can be nothing but organic. She waits, while the
Valerian drips to water, while he espouses energy scarcity and praises authors and
hypotheses. She hopes he will not confuse
pseudoscience with pseudo love.

Abigail Uhrick

The Inevitable After

There is acrimony here: choke
cherries and a hex key
are not the right tools
for this job. I have carried these
batteries in my pocketbook
for months now, but none will click
into any dead device.

We have seen the way the black
birds congregate around the rusted
parts as if there is flesh there. But
we are reasonably sure there is nothing
organic left. We cannot smell
the decay of previous days, nor can we
translate the clicking of the crows.
They are becoming so thick as to
obscure the fog. We have little time left
to discover some source or a different crop.

I will plead to stay inside and seal
what is left in jars—to wrap the windows
in foil and plastic. You will insist
on striking out towards a more fecund
destination—a spade in one hand and stones
of the last fruit in the other.

But the bees are long gone, and the flowers
we need are infrequent. The metal seems
to multiply when the birds have retired
from their manifold shifts. You cannot pull me from
this place, so we transfer into the next mode
of survival: staying. We have to discover now
how to be smarter than the machines
and learn to build
a better jam.

Abigail Uhrick

The Way of the Dodo

She is surprised on days
when the sparkles that fell off
glint in the rug or on your cheek when you
turn to look through her. It takes time
for her permanent shape to solidify enough
to block the morning sun; until then,
you just need to keep blotting the edges
with cloth.

The workers used to work but now only
put on suits and shined shoes to try to peer in
her windows to catch a glimpse
before she is whole or gone again. You are
a worker, too, and now it is your job to leave
her in the mornings anyway; you
have some looking in windows
of your own to do.

So she will grow whole less and then disintegrate a bit
more daily—the last of her clade. When you are out,
she will hop and shake to rid herself of the excess
weight of ancestry. She will pull the blinds down
to hide from the workers' witness and make
small piles of her molt for easier disposal.
Like those before her, she has no tongue, so she
cannot recount a history to be recorded.

While you are pressing your nose to the cold
glass of strangers, looking for others, she
is slowly fading. As everyone knows, once it starts,
there is no way to stop it: the lessening.
The workers brush lint from their sleeves, straighten
their seams, and move on. She is too long
or thin for even one egg. There is
little hope, if any. Poor, terrestrial bird.

Abigail Uhrick

Migration Diorama

There is no known plan for this infrastructure. What is inside cannot
be mapped with conventional methods.

Once a domicile, once a hall of worship, once an abandoned factory. Twice
a towering brick steeple, twice a precarious house of cards,

twice a complex connection of subway tunnels. Ten times a deer blind fastened
between maples, fifty times a wooden speed boat glossy with varnish.

One hundred times a non-descript receptacle. Never
an expansion bridge, never an earth ship, never an institution.

They will try to plot the points and notate all movement. They will attempt
to secure one point of reference from which to build

a model. They will think in terms of putty and paint, wood screws
and plasma. They won't be able to tack the configuration down to make their measure.

Biographies

Sybil Baker is the author of three books of fiction. She is a UC Foundation Assistant Professor at the University of Tennessee at Chattanooga and teaches at the Yale Writer's Conference. In 2015, she was Visiting Professor at Middle East Technical University in North Cyprus. She has been awarded two MakeWork Grants and a 2017 Individual Artists Fellowship from the Tennessee Arts Commission. She is Fiction Editor at *Drunken Boat. Immigration Essays,* is forthcoming in early 2017 from C&R Press

Terry Barr is the author of the essay collection, *Don't Date Baptists and Other Warnings From My Alabana Mother.* His work has appeared in *South Writ Large, Eclectica Magazine, Turk's Head Review,* and *Hippocampus,* among other journals. He lives in Greenville,South Carolina with his family.

Jorge Luis Borges is a very fine writer from Buenos Aires, Argentina. His fiction is exhilarating.

Ashley Chambers is a Master of Divinity candidate at Union Theological Seminary in NYC. She received her MFA in Creative Writing from the University of Alabama in 2015. Her writing appears in or is forthcoming from *Prelude, Salt Hill Journal, The Seattle Review,* among others. She was a finalist for the 2014 and 2015 Sawtooth Poetry Contests at Ahsahta Press and a finalist for Omnidawn's 2015 1st/2nd Poetry Book Prize. Her prose has received honorable mentions in fiction contests at *Gulf Coast* and *Bellevue Literary Review.* Her website is www.ashleyelizabethchambers.com.

Sheldon Lee Compton lives in Eastern Kentucky. His work has appeared in numerous journals and has been nominated for several awards, as well as anthologized on many occasions. He is a past founder and editor of three literary journals. He is the author of *The Same Terrible Storm* (Foxhead Books, 2012) and *Brown Bottle: A Novel* (Bottom Dog Press, 2016).

Jack D. Harvey's poetry has appeared in *Scrivener, Mind In Motion, Slow Dancer, The Antioch Review, Bay Area Poets' Coalition, The University of Texas Review, The Beloit Poetry Journal, The Piedmont Journal of Poetry,* and a number of other on-line and in print poetry magazines over the years, many of which are probably kaput by now, given the high mortality rate of poetry magazines. The author has been writing poetry since he was sixteen and lives in a small town near Albany, New York. He was born and worked in upstate New York. He is retired from doing whatever he was doing before he retired. He once owned a cat that could whistle "Sweet Adeline," use a knife and fork, and killed a postman.

Monica Hileman grew up in the Midwest, lived in the Pacific Northwest and settled in New England. Two years in Greensboro, North Carolina, yielded an MFA from UNC-G. Her stories have appeared in journals such as *Arts & Letters, The Baffler, the Chicago Tribune's Printers Row Journal,* and *South Dakota Review. Flyway: Journal of Writing & Environmen*t nominated an on-line story they published in 2015 for The Best of the Net.

Kaitlin Jennrich is an undergraduate student at Northwestern University. She has previously been published in *The Best Teen Writing of 2011.*

Carrie Meadows lives in Chattanooga, Tennessee, where she teaches creative, professional, and academic writing. Her work has appeared in *North American Review, Prairie Schooner, Mid-American Review,* and other publications. Her first poetry collection is forthcoming from Calypso Editions in 2017.

Charles O'Hay is the author of two collections—*Far from Luck* (2011) and *Smoking in Elevators* (2014)—both published by Lucky Bat Books. His work has appeared in over 140 literary publications including *The New York Quarterly, Cortland Review, Gargoyle, Riprap,* and *Pittsburgh Poetry Review.*

Chad Prevost holds a Ph.D. in creative writing from Georgia State. He is author of *A Frequency for Wherever You Are, Signs as Clues and*

Sometimes Wonders, The Blue Demon, White-Feathered Bodies, Chasing the Gods, and *Greatest Hits.* He has led workshops and panels at the Association of Writers and Writing Programs (AWP), Baylor University's Art and Soul Conference, Austin College, Clemson University, the Yale Writers' Conference, the Meacham Writers' Workshop, Lost in the Letters Festival, and for The Southern Collective. His writing has been in print in places such as *American Poetry Journal, Matter: A Journal of Compressed Creative Arts, North American Review, Mid-American Review, Prairie Schooner, Puerto del Sol, The Seattle Review, Sentence, The Southern Review* and *The Washington Post.* Chad lives in Chattanooga with his wife and their three children.

Sally Roundhouse is a poet living in Tucson, Arizona.

Robert Joe Stout is a freelance journalist, fiction writer and poet living in Oaxaca, Mexico. His most recent books are *Monkey Screams,* poetry from FutureCycle Press, and the novel *Where Gringos Don't Belong.*

Abigail Uhrick has worked as a technology consultant for a defense contractor, an editor for a niche publisher, and an instructor of business, technical, rhetorical, and creative writing at colleges in California and Michigan. She currently teaches in Northern Michigan. Her work has been published in *Hawai'i Pacific Review* and *Columbia Poetry Review* and is forthcoming in *Axolotl.*